THE GRAVY TRAIN

Also by Whit Masterson

THE DEATH OF ME YET
THE LAST ONE KILLS
PLAY LIKE YOU'RE DEAD
711—OFFICER NEEDS HELP
MAN ON A NYLON STRING
EVIL COME, EVIL GO
A HAMMER IN HIS HAND
THE DARK FANTASTIC
A SHADOW IN THE WILD
BADGE OF EVIL
ALL THROUGH THE NIGHT
DEAD, SHE WAS BEAUTIFUL

THE GRAVY TRAIN

Whit Masterson

A RED BADGE NOVEL OF SUSPENSE

DODD, MEAD & COMPANY · NEW YORK

To Col. James Allison Moore, USAF (ret.),

a lifelong idol without feet of clay

Copyright © 1971 by Whit Masterson
All rights reserved
No part of this book may be reproduced in any form
without permission in writing from the publisher

ISBN 0-396-06320-9
Library of Congress Catalog Card Number: 74-145398
Printed in the United States of America
by Vail-Ballou Press, Inc., Binghamton, N. Y.

ONE

> Hub McBain was a proud engineer,
> A highballin' man who didn't know fear,
> The best pig mauler from here to Maine,
>   The iron he drove was The Gravy Train.
>
> Hub raced the best and he licked 'em too
> (There was some who claimed he really flew!),
> From hell to breakfast and back again,
>   In that iron they called The Gravy Train.
>
> Now Hub had grit and a heap of pride,
> Wasn't a man who could match his stride.
> Swore he'd whip God too if He would deign,
>   To race with Hub and The Gravy Train.
>
> —The Ballad of The Gravy Train

In the United States, prisons tend to look like factories. In Latin America, they tend to look like castles and often present a picturesque, even romantic appearance, a description which can scarcely be applied to Sing Sing or San Quentin.

El Castillo de San Angelo near Cartagena, Colombia, is routinely pointed out to tourists as a splendid example of Spanish colonial architecture. Guardian of the Carribbean port through which the wealth of the New World flowed to the Old, the four-hundred-year-old fort looks formidable even today. Its thick stone walls were designed to resist the heaviest bombardment. Huge cannon stood on the battlements, their blunt snouts poked through the twelve embrasures named for the apostles. High merlons shielded the defenders from salvos by hostile warships. A deep moat made attack from the landward side equally difficult. Yet for all of this, Cartagena was sacked on several occasions by pirates under flags both lawful and unlawful. When Barranquilla to the north became Spain's principal Atlantic port, San Angelo was abandoned for military purposes. In the latter part of the nineteenth century, Colombia's new masters refurbished it as a prison to house their political opponents. The towering gray walls had not kept pirates out; they did keep criminals in. In the jargon of penology, San Angelo was termed a maximum security facility. Its involuntary residents coined a more graphic description: La Tumba, the tomb. Few escaped and not many more managed to serve out their sentences, giving rise to the saying that there were only two ways to leave La Tumba, head first or feet first, depending on which way the coffin was pointed.

In more recent times, Colombia was able to claim that La Tumba, while austere, was far from the dungeon it had once been. Prisoners were no longer brutalized, starved or allowed to rot with disease. Rather, they were given an adequate diet and excellent medical care, employed productively (La Tumba turned out several thousand pairs of sandals each month) and permitted certain limited privileges.

Among those privileges was one common to most Latin American prisons but which scandalizes visitors from the north, the conjugal visit. The Puritan ethic holds sex as sinful or, at best, a weakness. The Latin views sex as an essential function of the human animal. To deny a man sexual activity simply because he is a prisoner strikes him as both cruel and irrational; nature will be served, one way or another. Wives are not only permitted but encouraged to maintain normal marital relations with their husbands for the physical and emotional benefit of both. If this strikes the Yankee as coddling, the Latin can point out that sodomy and other perversions rampant in U.S. penitentiaries are little practiced in his.

Yet every system, however admirable, has its drawbacks. As the Colombians put it: *No hay rosas sin espinas,* there are no roses without thorns. Prisoners have been known to attempt escape in women's clothing smuggled in by their wives. The trick is now an old one and the guards are rarely fooled by it, particularly at a maximum security facility such as El Castillo de San Angelo.

On a humid afternoon late in December, four orange-colored buses stood outside the walls of La Tumba, engines idling as they waited for the last of their passengers to be passed by the inspection. Every Sunday morning the buses rumbled through Cartagena and the neighboring villages, collecting their female cargo. Every Sunday evening they returned, *el día de la familia* over. Most of the wives made the trip weekly; many had left homes elsewhere and settled in and around Cartagena in order to be near their men. Others commuted regularly but less frequently from more distant points. Only those making the pilgrimage for the first time betrayed any embarrassment. Filing out the iron gate, they chatted and laughed like women anywhere and gave the guards the same casual farewell they had given their husbands a few minutes earlier— *Hasta luego,* until next time.

Sergeant Hector Gallardo leaned against the wall of the tunnel, sweating and replying to the good-bys with a bored nod. As the last of the wives passed, he lit a cigarillo and flipped the match toward the other guard. "The count?"

Corporal Lopez looked up from his clipboard. "Ninety-six in. Ninety-six out." He winked. "I was wagering that it would be ninety-six in, ninety-seven out. Did you see Señora Herrera? Big as a house—she must be a month overdue. Has there ever been a baby born in La Tumba, I wonder?"

"Not to my knowledge. God only knows how many have been made here, however. But that's none of your business, Lopez, or mine. Your business is to count. Mine is to certify that you have counted correctly."

While Gallardo verified the tally, the younger guard mused, "They say that a child born in a foreign embassy automatically becomes a citizen of that country. Would then a child born in La Tumba automatically become a prisoner?"

"We are all prisoners in one fashion or another. You, me, the men in their cells—even the child in Señora Herrera's womb. What is life except a sentence?" Gallardo scrawled his name at the bottom of the tally sheet. "The count is accurate. Inform the drivers that they may depart."

As Lopez moved indolently to obey, there was a shout. Turning, they saw the silhouette of a man sprinting toward them down the dim tunnel. Gallardo, recognizing the uniform of an officer if not its wearer, stiffened to attention. In the same motion he dropped the forbidden cigarillo to the pavement and covered it with his boot.

The officer responded to the salute with a mere flick of his fingers. "Lieutenant Villa, security detail," he panted with obvious agitation. "The wives—have they left yet?"

"I only this moment completed verifying the count. As the Lieutenant knows, the drivers are under orders not to depart until—"

"Thank God! One of the prisoners is missing. The Yankee colonel, Heaston. We suspect that he is attempting to escape disguised as a woman."

"Impossible! I mean, sir, that the tally checks. Ninety-six in, ninety-six out. Examine it for yourself."

Lieutenant Villa gave the clipboard a scornful glance. "Marks on paper, Sergeant. They mean nothing. Are you prepared to swear that all of the ninety-six are actually women?"

Gallardo hesitated. "Naturally, we don't examine—"

"Precisely. You see a skirt and a mantilla and assume the wearer is female. It wouldn't be the first time that incompetent guards have fallen for that ruse." Villa snapped his fingers in the direction of the buses. "Order the women to get out and return to the Sala de Armas for my inspection. I guarantee that I am able to tell the difference between the sexes."

Gallardo flushed at the rebuke, but he made the only reply permitted by discipline. "Yes, sir!" He took out his resentment on his subordinate. "Why are you standing there with your mouth open? You heard the Lieutenant's orders!"

Lopez, trotting to match his angry strides, whispered, "What reason do we give them, Sergeant? They're certain to raise a fuss."

"Tell them to complain to the lieutenant. Damn these new officers! You know and I know that the Yankee didn't slip by us, but because we're only stupid enlisted men . . ." Gallardo stuck his head into the open door of the first bus and shouted, "Everyone out! Return to the prison immediately!"

Lopez was correct in predicting that the order would cause commotion. A loud chorus of questions and complaints greeted it. Gallardo paid no attention. By the time he repeated the command for the final bus, women were erupting from the others like angry bees from a hive. They swarmed about the two guards, demanding an explanation. When it was supplied, tersely, a fresh storm of indignation broke out. Inspection? Ridiculous! Strip in front of grinning males? Unthinkable! Gallardo, besieged, promised them (and hoped he wasn't lying) that no such indignities were contemplated. A few questions to establish their identities would suffice. If the good señoras would only cooperate, it would be easier on all concerned.

Some of the good señoras continued to breathe defiance. A few attempted to get back aboard the buses. The majority, their annoyance vented, adopted a let's-get-it-over-with attitude and began to file across the moat. Gallardo instructed Lopez to keep the line moving and elbowed his way to its head, seeking the officer responsible for the turmoil.

He encountered another officer instead, no stranger, but a veteran of La Tumba. Captain Garcia stood in the middle of the narrow tunnel like a rock in a stream while the exasperated female tide flowed by on both sides.

"What is the meaning of this?" he demanded. "Why are they coming back, Sergeant? And what is this babble about an inspection?"

"Lieutenant Villa's orders," Gallardo explained, glad to be able to fix the blame where it belonged. "The women are to be examined to make certain that one is not the escaped prisoner."

"What escaped prisoner? I've heard nothing about it. There must be some mistake."

"Lieutenant Villa was very positive, sir. The Yankee colonel, Heaston, he said, the one who—"

"I know Colonel Heaston well. It's this Lieutenant—

Villa, did you say?—whom I don't know. Where is he?"

"I assume he's already in the Sala, preparing for the inspection."

"He's not. I just came from there." Garcia's eyes narrowed. "Describe this Villa for me."

"A tall man, well set up, every inch an officer, if you know what I mean, although a bit old for a lieutenant—"

"How old? Fifty, perhaps? Field grade age?"

Gallardo stared in sudden consternation. "But that's impossible," he stammered. "I, too, know the Yankee. He has a full beard—"

"Which he could have shaved off in approximately the same amount of time it took him to put on the lieutenant's uniform. You consummate ass! Quickly—he can't have gotten far!"

He plunged into the female torrent, fighting toward the gate with Gallardo at his heels, oblivious to the voices chiding their discourtesy. Lopez was shepherding the last of the wives into the tunnel while being harangued from behind by the bus drivers, who were no less indignant at the delay than their passengers.

"Captain, will you kindly inform these gentlemen that it is not I who am responsible for—"

"The lieutenant!" Garcia growled, seizing his arm and shaking him like a naughty child. "What has become of the lieutenant, you moron?"

"The lieutenant?" Lopez echoed in bewilderment. "How should I know, sir?"

"You have eyes, haven't you? Which way did he go?" Garcia gave him another shake, then pushed him roughly away. "Search the buses; he may be hiding in one of them. Sergeant, sound the alarm, order out two squads on the double." As Gallardo darted off, he wheeled on the drivers. "And you—clear the road by getting your vehicles away from the gates immediately."

"We can't," one of the drivers told him. "The lieutenant confiscated the keys. He promised we'd get them back when the inspection was over."

"And you permitted it?" Garcia asked in a strangled voice.

"He was very forceful, Captain. One does not argue with authority. I confess I thought it strange when I saw him get into the truck, but—"

"What truck?"

"The one parked across the moat. Naturally, I assumed it was a prison vehicle."

"You assumed! Gallardo assumed! And while you jackasses were occupied with your assuming, Colonel Heaston slipped through your fingers!" Garcia's pudgy body quivered with rage. "Lopez, get a complete description of the truck—model, color, body type, license if anyone can remember it. I'll notify the police in Cartagena to seize it before it can leave the area." He grimaced as a fresh thought struck him. "Unless, of course, that Yankee devil has also managed to cut the telephone wires."

In the back of the lurching truck, Anthony Heaston was stripping off the lieutenant's tunic when he heard the distant wail of the prison siren. "Tallyho, chaps," he murmured. With no watch to verify it, he could only estimate the time between escape and discovery as five minutes. Not much of a margin, but with luck it should be enough—although Heaston had long since ceased to believe in luck, good, bad or otherwise. Luck was a false idol by which men absolved themselves of responsibility; it made defeat acceptable and victory hollow. His own negligence, not luck, had confined him to La Tumba in the first place. His own resourcefulness, not luck, had permitted him to escape it.

If escape he had; the next half-hour would decide.

He began to don the clothing—shirt, tie, gray and white seersucker suit—which the suitcase contained. It was difficult to stand to put on the trousers. The truck, with a fine disregard for the potholes which pitted the road, maintained a breakneck pace, and the low canvas roof forced him into a crouch. Though on the threshold of fifty, his lean muscular body possessed the supple grace of a man thirty years younger (again not luck, but methodical exercise even during his imprisonment). No amount of determination had prevented gray from creeping into his hair, but it was still luxuriant and nearly as black as the deep-set eyes. They clashed with the unnatural whiteness of his face, the pallor of the sickroom and the cell. Heaston used the tube of tanning lotion to restore the skin to its normal brown. He attached a false mustache to complete the transformation and rapped on the window that separated him from the cab. The swarthy driver did not slow down or glance around but waved a hand in acknowledgment. The truck continued to race past groves of coco palms and fields of sugar cane.

Suddenly it swerved, with only a slight reduction of speed, and left the highway for another even more wretched. Heaston recognized that they had entered Tesca Swamp, the marshland northeast of the city. Mahogany and cedar and brazilwood trees grew thickly on both sides of the road, little better than a trail, their branches meeting to form a canopy above it. Guadua bamboo brushed the sides of the truck as it passed. They slowed to a crawl. The driver sounded his horn three times. Two answering beeps came from somewhere close by. The truck ground to a stop. Heaston vaulted over the tailgate. Before he had regained his balance, the truck lurched away again, a belch of exhaust fumes its only farewell.

A sleek black sedan containing two men waited in the concealment of the bamboo thicket, engine idling, one door open invitingly. Heaston flung himself in beside the driver.

The man behind the wheel gave him a jaunty salute. "Welcome aboard, Colonel." He was a red-haired American of about forty, powerfully built, with the neck and torso of a bull. Or perhaps a bear; his arms were stubby and his legs short, hardly long enough to permit his feet to reach the pedals. There was an animal-like quality to the face also, not a lack of intelligence, but of human warmth, an effect heightened by the opaque eyes which seldom seemed to blink. "Guess I don't need to ask how things went, seeing you're here right on schedule."

"It worked perfectly—with a little help from my friends, of course." Heaston squeezed the thick shoulder affectionately. "God, but you're a beautiful sight, Bronko!"

"Told you there was nothing to worry about," Bronko said to the man who sat silently in the rear of the sedan. "Colonel, say hello to Mr. Zeus."

Heaston extended his hand. Mr. Zeus clasped it nervously. He was American also, slender to the point of gauntness, Heaston's age or older, to judge by the silver hair. He wore a lightweight suit of expensive silk; there was a diamond on his finger and a scarlet feather in the brim of his panama hat. Wraparound sun glasses hid most of his florid face. Heaston murmured, "So you're my fairy godfather, eh? I'm delighted to find out I actually have one."

"And I'm delighted to see that Bronko didn't exaggerate your ingenuity," Mr. Zeus replied in a voice which carried the hint of a lisp. "Congratulations on your escape, Colonel."

"It goes without saying that I'm deeply grateful to you.

Sorry I didn't get a chance to thank my driver, too. Who was he, by the way?"

"Local talent," Bronko explained, pointing the sedan back toward the main highway. "He's already been thanked plenty—in pesos. He'll ditch the truck in the swamp. By the time the cops figure out they're looking for the wrong car, we'll be on the plane."

"Might be wiser for me to lie low for a few days. They're bound to be checking outgoing flights."

"Not ours," Mr. Zeus told him. "It's all been arranged. More pesos, Colonel. Money speaks the same language everywhere. Only the accent varies."

"Your new passport's in the glove compartment," Bronko added. "Better look it over, get familiar with yourself just in case."

Heaston glanced from one to the other of his rescuers, his expression quizzical. "Just one question. Where's the fire?"

"Fire?" repeated Mr. Zeus.

"The one I'm supposed to start—or put out, as the case may be. I can't imagine any other reason why you'd go to all the time, trouble and expense to salvage an old soldier from the scrap heap."

"Perhaps we couldn't abide the idea of allowing the legendary Colonel Anthony Heaston to rot away in a South American prison."

Heaston grinned. "Now why the hell didn't I think of that?"

The limousine deposited him at the side entrance to Walter Reed Hospital, which was often referred to as the Brass Gate. George Upp bounded up the steps, shielded by the porte-cochère from the pelting February rain but not from the chill wind whipping off the Potomac. The guard detail snapped crisply to attention. Although Upp wore civilian clothes, he possessed the unmistakable bearing of the general officer; he carried his stars in his face rather than on his shoulders.

The orderly at the desk inside responded in the same fashion. "The General's expecting you, sir. Suite 201, second floor, end of the corridor."

Scorning the elevator, Upp took the stairs two steps at a time and was gratified to find he could manage it easily. At sixty-three, he was as trim as the day he left the Point and weighed not a pound more. Now as then, he ran a mile every morning; his sport was rowing, not golf. If he was known to irreverent subordinates as the Silver Fox, it was less a reference to his steel gray mane than a tribute to his position atop the nation's intelligence community.

Edith Carson answered his knock. "George!" she said warmly, taking his hands with the almost girlish cordiality that had made her a beloved First Lady. "So very good of you to come." Seventy years had turned the black hair snow white and the anxiety of recent months had added new lines to the patrician face. Yet neither age nor worry could completely extinguish the vivacity of the one-time Savannah belle. She had entered Walter Reed to be near her husband, the ailing ex-President, and made a home of it as she had done everywhere, wars permitting, that duty had led him.

"Sorry I couldn't get here sooner. My flight was delayed. Some nut phoned that there was a bomb aboard and we had to turn back. False alarm, of course."

Edith shuddered. "Weren't you simply petrified? I swear nobody's ever going to get me aboard one of those awful contraptions. Orrin says I'm chicken, but I say better a live chicken than a dead duck."

"Cut it out, Edith," Upp admonished with a smile.

"You've got more guts than any ten men. Tell me, how is the General?"

"About the same." She hesitated. "Well, maybe a little weaker—but the doctors say that's only to be expected. All the cobalt treatment, you know. He'll be delighted to see you." She led him across the suite to the door to the adjoining bedroom. It stood ajar; Edith peeked around it. "Honey, you decent? George Upp is here." The reply was a growl Upp knew well. Edith gave his hand a final squeeze and a mock warning. "Call if you need help."

Upp smiled back. Yet he entered the sickroom with the concealed apprehension that a summons from the General had always aroused. Orrin Kell Carson—known affectionately to millions the world over as O.K.—was propped up in the high bed. A microphone hung around his neck, its cord extending to the tape recorder on the table. More conventional hospital paraphernalia surrounded him also, a green tank of oxygen, a portable EKG console and the tall pole which held the intravenous equipment, while a plastic tent formed a canopy above the bed. None of the devices was presently employed, since the patient's condition was considered serious but not critical.

Upp had not seen his old commander-in-chief since he had entered Walter Reed the previous November. He was shocked at the deterioration he beheld. The cancer against which O.K. had fought so long was obviously winning. The wasted figure held little resemblance to the vigorous dynamic leader under whom Upp had served. Nevertheless, he made his greeting cheerful. "General, you're looking great. You'll be back on the golf course in another month."

"Horse manure," the salty old soldier replied amiably. "You're nearly as bad a liar as Edith. I've got a mirror, and even if I didn't . . . At ease, George. Pull up a chair."

"I hope I didn't pick an inconvenient time, sir."

"No time's inconvenient when you don't have much left." O.K. tapped the microphone on his chest. "Dictating the final volume of my memoirs. Matter of fact, that's all I'm sticking around for. Never could stand to leave a job unfinished. Another month should be enough." He added with a wink, "The medics are betting I don't make it."

"I'd like a piece of that bet. You're good for years yet."

"I'll settle for the month." O.K. shifted irritably, seeking a more comfortable position and not finding it. "I sometimes wonder why I bother, though. Sheer vanity, I suppose. The family doesn't need the money. The royalties, if any, will go to fund that damn Memorial and Library back home in Alamogordo. Don't know how I ever allowed myself to be talked into that project in the first place. More vanity. Course, I didn't believe I ever was going to die. Now that I know better, I'd be a lot happier with six feet of grass over at Arlington instead of umpteen tons of New Mexico pink marble. A man should have a grave, not a bloody shrine."

"There are millions of Americans who wouldn't agree with you," Upp told him sincerely. "You mean a lot to them, General. It's only natural that they want to give you that final honor. Even the kids, chipping in their nickels and dimes . . . The Memorial isn't a monument to your vanity. It's our way of saying thanks."

"You sound like you're bucking for promotion, George. Doesn't the USIB satisfy you?"

"Can't complain, sir. Though I'll admit running the Intelligence Board isn't half as much fun as when I was your G-2. Those were the good old days."

"Yeah," O.K. murmured, his eyes fixed on events long past. Then he snorted. "Who are we kidding? The only good thing about the good old days is that they're over. We cussed them plenty at the time, as I recall."

"Distance lends enchantment," Upp agreed smiling. "All the same, we had a hell of a time."

"Speaking of the old days, good or bad—I wonder if you happen to remember a chap named Heaston."

His tone was casual but Upp, knowing him, recognized that the question was not. Carson, despite his outward bluff simplicity, frequently demonstrated an Oriental deviousness, a combination which had brought him success in politics as well as war. Upp suspected that they were at last getting around to the reason he had been summoned to the sickbed. Faithful to his training, he replied to the question and asked none of his own. "I could scarcely forget Mad Anthony."

"That's the rascal. One of the best guerrilla leaders the Army ever produced, part Francis Marion, part Bedford Forrest—with a dash of Custer thrown in."

"More than just a dash, in my opinion. Closer to a gallon."

"Whatever the proportions, you can't deny that Heaston had a certain genius." O.K. sighed. "And all wasted. A colonel before he was thirty, headed for the top. At fifty, a paid mercenary, little better than a pirate, leading revolutions and cutting throats for anyone with the dirty money to pay him. Sad, sad. I blame myself to some extent, George."

"You shouldn't, sir. You did the right thing."

"The expedient thing," O.K. corrected. "There's often a difference. If I'd handled Heaston's case the right way fifteen years ago, instead of the expedient way . . ."

Upp still failed to perceive what the ex-President was driving at; certainly it could not be to deplore past mistakes. "Personally, I have no regrets. Heaston was a dangerous man—brilliant, I grant you, charming, too, but with no more principles than a weasel in a hen house. The United States is well rid of him."

"Are we?" O.K. murmured, his fingers toying with the microphone cord. "Rid of him, I mean."

"Heaston is serving a life term down in Colombia for leading that revolt that fizzled a couple of years ago."

"It pains me to correct the head of USIB," O.K. said slyly, "but my intelligence is superior to yours. Tony Heaston broke out of prison around Christmas. He's been back in the States since January, according to the CIA. I was dealing with the Do Binh affair for the book and asked them for an update on Heaston's career since then."

"I must remember to compliment the CIA on keeping me informed."

"Oh, you know how it goes. They undoubtedly didn't consider the matter important enough to buck up to your rarefied atmosphere."

"But you do," Upp said slowly. "What's worrying you, General?"

"Heaston. Colombia claims that his escape was engineered by foreign interests, that it was well planned and heavily financed. For what purpose? Obviously, to use him in some sordid adventure of the type he's infamous for."

"That certainly sounds logical. As you say, the man's little better than a pirate. But I'm not sure I see—"

"Why I'm getting my bowels in an uproar? Call it a hunch, even call it senility if you like, but I can't shake off the feeling . . ." O.K. made a scrubbing motion with his palm, familiar to Upp from many a strategy session, as if clearing a fogged glass in order to perceive what lay beyond. "Heaston's not one for petty projects. In the past what he did hasn't been any real concern to us because he did it somewhere else. But now, after fifteen years, Heaston has started to play in our yard. I think it behooves us to find out why."

"Have you considered the possibility that Colombia is exaggerating about his escape to whitewash their own negligence? Saving face, as it were."

"Yes. I've also considered the possibility that Heaston is merely homesick for the good old U.S.A. I can't buy either one. Can you?"

"Perhaps not, sir. On the other hand, to be truthful about it, I can't see Heaston representing any real danger to this country, either. After all, he's just one man."

"So was Lee Harvey Oswald." He took note of Upp's incredulous expression. "Hell, I'm not suggesting Heaston means to assassinate the President. That's not his style. But there's plenty of other mischief that is. Don't ever underestimate the potential of the individual, George—for either good or evil. We people in government, and particularly the military, get so used to thinking in terms of the mass that we forget everything from Christianity to Communism began with just one man."

"Yes, sir." Upp cleared his throat. "What would you like me to do?"

"Damn it, do I have to draw you a picture? Find out what Heaston's up to, of course." O.K. tempered his curtness with a grin. "That's not an order, much as it sounds like it. I don't give orders any more. Hard habit to break, though. Let's say I'm asking a favor instead."

"I'll put someone on it right away," Upp told him, feeling a rush of sentiment for his old comrade, gallantly fighting his last battle. He could not share O.K.'s exaggerated apprehension concerning Anthony Heaston, but he was happy to indulge him in it, a small kindness certainly. And —perhaps—he felt a secret relief that Carson desired nothing more demanding of him; dying requests are frequently burdensome.

There was a knock on the corridor door. A medical team entered without waiting to be bid. "Sixteen hundred hours," the doctor announced with professional cheeriness. "That time again, General. Feel like giving us another blood sample?"

"Didn't I give you enough yesterday?" O.K. grumbled.

"Well, sir, like the man says—what have you done for us lately?" The doctor turned his smile in Upp's direction. "If you wouldn't mind stepping into the next room—"

Upp thought the moment propitious to take his leave. "I have to be running along, anyway. It's been great talking with you, General."

"I'll expect your report on that matter," O.K. called after him.

"I'll deliver it personally," Upp promised. But he reflected somberly that his visit had ended as it had begun, with a kindly lie. He doubted if he would ever see O.K. Carson again, except at his funeral.

The Federal Bureau of Investigation's headquarters on Constitution Avenue maintains its own cafeteria for its employees. The food is palatable, the prices moderate. However, as Jacob Duffy put it with customary impudence, when the boss is buying, might as well go first cabin. So his steak this particular afternoon was filet, not Swiss, and his goblet held imported Chablis, not tap water.

"That was excellent, F.X. Thanks for suggesting we eat here."

His companion chuckled wryly. "All I remember suggesting was that we grab a quiet bite somewhere. Some bite —twelve-fifty for lunch! That's going to look great on the old expense account." His name was Francis Xavier Raymond, usually shortened to F.X. by his intimates and often to X-Ray by his subordinates. The nickname was a tribute to his piercing blue eyes, which legend had it could see through a wall or an alibi with equal ease. He was a chipper plump man of fifty-five whose ruddy face and horseshoe of white hair made his resemble Hollywood's stereotype of the Irish priest. However, Raymond dealt with another sort of confession. He was the assistant director of the FBI and its representative on the USIB, that elite group which serves as the steering committee for the federal government's intelligence agencies. Picking up the check, he suggested slyly, "Match you for it, Jake?"

"I never gamble," Duffy replied piously. "Against regulations, you know."

"So are those sideburns and that Fu Manchu mustache. I don't notice that stops you from wearing them."

"It's a Zapata mustache. The Fu Manchu is longer, curves down around the mouth. Anyway, wearing the hair short is a Bureau custom, not a regulation. I checked."

"I'll bet you did at that. Never miss a trick, do you?"

"If you can't be brilliant, be thorough," Duffy agreed with the patently false modesty of a man who is both and knows it. He was thirty-two but looked younger, a strikingly handsome dark-haired man with a graceful carriage and well-modulated voice which often caused strangers to assume he was an actor or, more recently (glancing at the facial hair), a graduate student. Both estimates were partially correct. Duffy's job required him to play a variety of roles but never on a stage; he had spent the past six months enrolled in not one college but several. His true title—inspector, Special Assignments Division—was little known outside the Bureau. Duffy himself rarely used it since Special Assignments was a euphemism for undercover work.

Raymond dropped his bantering tone. "Any questions about your new case?"

"Yes. Why me? Now don't tell me, F.X. Let me guess. There's no one else in the Bureau qualified to handle this assignment, right? Wrong. You think I've earned a vacation, right? Wrong again. You're getting me out of Washington before the Chief remembers who recommended me to head up SAD, right? Right."

Raymond's blue eyes glinted with amusement. "Let's say that I think both Washington and Jake Duffy will profit from a temporary separation. You seem to be making a career out of antagonizing the power structure. I'd like to remind you that in government service, that adds up to no career at all." He ticked off the evidence on his stubby fingers. "First, your investigation into union hiring practices which drove certain labor bosses straight up the wall. Next, the probe into kickbacks on defense contracts which started certain prime contractors hollering for your scalp. And now your report on the student protest movement—"

"All my report said was that the students are frequently right in what they want, usually wrong in the way they try to get it—and that there's not one shred of evidence pointing to any international Communist conspiracy."

"Thereby infuriating all and pleasing none, including the Chief."

"I'm not running for Mr. Congeniality. I just do my job. And—since you force me to say so myself—better than anyone else."

"That's the only reason I've been able to protect you. There are plenty of people in this town who are just waiting for you to make that one big mistake so they can bounce you out on your big fat ego."

"They should know by now that I don't make mistakes, big or little."

Raymond regarded him for a moment. "Your record has been phenomenal. But don't start thinking you're God.

Listen to me seriously, boy. You've got the best mind in the Bureau, bar none, and I don't want to lose you. But unless I can teach you a little humility—"

"Am I to assume that finding this Colonel Whozis is lesson number one?"

"The name is Heaston—Anthony Heaston. I guess you're too young to remember him. He had one of the first units sent into Vietnam—we were calling them advisers in those days—to train the South to deal with the guerrillas. Actually, they did more fighting than advising. Heaston's Hellions, no better soldiers anywhere. Trouble is, even the best soldiers need to operate under a clear-cut directive. By maintaining the fiction that they were merely advisers, confusion arose who was actually calling the shots. Was it the U.S. Army? The South Vietnamese? The CIA? Or was it Heaston himself? Now the political situation in Vietnam at the time—" He broke off to eye Duffy sternly. "I may ask questions later."

"I'm paying attention, F.X. The political situation in Vietnam at the time—"

"Yeah. Well, the Saigon regime had something less than overwhelming popular support. Without our backing, it wouldn't have lasted a week. The leader of the local opposition was a chap named Do Binh. The regime claimed Do Binh was working for Hanoi and ordered Colonel Heaston to arrest him. Next thing you know, Do Binh is dead. Shot while attempting to escape was the official story. But then the rumor got around that he'd really been executed."

"Had he?"

"Possibly. The only fact that everyone could agree on was that Do Binh was dead and that Heaston's Hellions had killed him. Faced with a sticky situation, our Southeast Asia Command overreacted. To prove its hands were clean, they charged Heaston and a dozen of his men with murder and brought them home to face a court-martial—probably the stupidest move they could have made. Heaston's best and logical defense was that whatever he did, he did under orders, which immediately raises the question: Who gave the orders? It promised to be a very embarrassing trial. The State Department was unhappy, the CIA was unhappy, Saigon was unhappy . . . so President Carson stepped in and ordered the charges dropped for lack of evidence. Do Binh's widow was indemnified with the princely sum of five thousand bucks. End of incident. Oh, there were the predictable cries of coverup and whitewash and some sentiment for a congressional investigation, but it blew over as it usually does."

"So the widow got the cash, the governments got off the hook. . . . What did Heaston get?"

"Screwed. Since the charges were dropped, Heaston never was convicted of anything. But he never was cleared, either. Ruined his career, naturally. They assigned him a desk in some dark corner of the Pentagon, gave him a flock of piddling jobs a PFC could handle . . . until he finally did what everybody hoped he would do, resign his commission and get lost."

"I'm surprised he didn't write a book. Everyone else seems to."

"The past dozen years he's been following his trade wherever they needed a good guerrilla—Africa, the Middle East, most recently South America. Two years ago he was involved in an attempt to overthrow the government in Colombia. The revolt fizzled, Heaston was captured and sentenced to life in prison. A couple of days after Christmas, he broke out."

"Any idea where he is now?"

"No. We know that he returned to the States in early

January with a man named Bronko Shaman. Shaman was Heaston's first sergeant and one of the twelve who were charged along with him in the Do Binh affair. Shaman apparently had something to do with springing his old CO out of the poky. Why? That's the question you're supposed to answer."

"Damned if I can see the point in hounding the man. We don't intend to send him back to Colombia, do we?"

"Even if we wanted to, Colombia wouldn't accept him. Just between us, George Upp suspects that O.K. has a guilt complex because he never gave Heaston his day in court. Since it's too late for that, the only way he can clear his conscience is by demonstrating that Heaston is now—and, consequently, always has been—a thoroughly rotten apple."

"And the Administration can hardly refuse a dying request from its patron saint, can it?"

"Politics do have a way of edging into the picture. For that reason, the matter must be handled discreetly. Make that very discreetly. The Administration doesn't care to have the Do Binh case revived, particularly in an election year. They'll be delighted if your investigation adds up to zero, even if O.K. isn't."

"In other words, the Bureau's best brain—quoting you, F.X.—is supposed to locate a man who isn't doing anything . . . and then report back that he isn't doing it."

"That's it exactly." Raymond grinned. "Think you can handle it?"

Duffy began by running the two names through the FBI scanner. The first drew a blank; Anthony Heaston had no record with any of the nation's law enforcement agencies. The second name was more productive. Bronko Shaman had departed the service with a bad conduct discharge. His civilian career since substantiated the military judgment. His dossier was studded with arrests on charges ranging from bookmaking and extortion to aggravated assault and forcible rape. Yet here, as in the Army, outside forces had moved to thwart justice; in each instance the charges had been dropped. Shaman's advancement in the army of the underworld had been steady if not meteoric. From union goon on the New York waterfront, his first job, to security boss for a Las Vegas casino, his latest, the former first sergeant of Heaston's Hellions had demonstrated the ability not only to survive but to prosper. In a sense, Bronko Shaman was still the expert guerrilla, operating behind enemy lines.

At the Pentagon, Duffy's next source, the situation was reversed. He was able to obtain a good deal of background on Heaston, but next to nothing on Shaman. The Army kept an open file on all officers, active or inactive, but not former enlisted men except those in the reserve. It was all there on microfilm, from inoculations to decorations (an almost equal number of both), commands held and campaigns waged, personality evaluation and medical history. The biography was out-of-date, as was the photograph which accompanied it; nothing had been added since Heaston's resignation from the service.

The Central Intelligence Agency presumably could have supplied chapter and verse on Heaston's activities during the past decade, but Duffy's query went unanswered. He was neither surprised nor dismayed. The CIA tended to regard the FBI as a competitor rather than an ally.

The information he already possessed was sufficient, anyway. Studying it, Duffy was struck by the similarity between the aging soldier of fortune and himself; Heaston might almost have been his elder brother. Both had known poverty and estrangement in childhood; each had chosen government service as the ladder to the top. By heredity mavericks, by nature egotists, neither had given the Establishment cause to love him, while at the same time acknowledging his value.

There were differences, of course, aside from the obvious ones of years and physical appearance. The charismatic colonel possessed a panache the sardonic investigator lacked. Yet the key difference was implicit rather than explicit. Heaston's almost suicidal gallantry showed him to be a fatalist, a creature moving in response to some whimsical destiny. Duffy, who could not accept destiny, whimsical or otherwise, believed only in himself. If Anthony Heaston's credo could be summed up as "Defy the gods and to hell with the consequences," then Jacob Duffy's credo was "Make no mistakes and to hell with the gods."

But, while Duffy might feel a certain kinship for the older man, circumstances had placed them in opposite camps, one the pursuer, the other the pursued—not necessarily enemies but unlikely to be friends. Duffy's only lead to his quarry's present whereabouts was the knowledge that Heaston had returned to the United States via Pan-American World Airways, Mexico City to Los Angeles. Since Pan-Am also flew to Houston, from whence connecting flights could be booked to eastern and middle western cities, Heaston's choice argued that the far west was his destination. When you added the fact that Las Vegas was Bronko Shaman's last reported place of employment . . .

Ordinarily, a teletype to the Las Vegas office of the FBI would have produced the information he sought, positive or negative. But locating Anthony Heaston was only half of the assignment. The other half, equally important though unofficial, was Raymond's desire that the chase should serve as a cooling-off period. Duffy booked passage on the first available flight to the Nevada resort city.

Raymond had not directed him to choose the most expensive lodgings in Las Vegas, of course. But neither had he forbid it. Duffy checked into the Xanadu, the latest gaudy addition to the already gaudy Strip.

He had two reasons for his choice. The first was that he enjoyed luxury, and the Xanadu was a palace worthy of its name. The gleaming white-and-gold hotel towered high above the desert floor like an obelisk erected to celebrate the triumph of hedonism. The opulent theater-restaurant on the top floor provided the best entertainment in town and the best view as well. The ground-floor casino made gambling seem not a vice to be indulged but a religion to be practiced. The Xanadu was owned by Julian Loud; some claimed it was his home. Where Loud was involved, you could never be absolutely certain of anything. He was generally referred to by the press as "the billionaire recluse," since Loud ran his international empire of interlocking companies—oil, shipping, petrochemicals, aerospace—behind a smoke screen through which he was rarely if ever seen. Secrecy invites rumors, and rumors are usually unreliable. If accounts of his Byzantine dealings were exaggerated, still there appeared little doubt that Julian Loud exerted considerable clout in politics as well as finance, both domestically and elsewhere. And if that clout was sometimes employed with questionable legality, no government had the evidence or the temerity to challenge him. Loud owned the Xanadu, but had not built it. He was by nature an acquirer rather than a builder. He collected corporations as he collected beautiful women, rare art and vintage aircraft, price no object. What he wanted he bought, often seemingly on whim as a child buys toys.

Duffy's second reason for choosing the Xanadu was the more important of the two. Bronko Shaman had been—and perhaps still was?—chief of security, the private police force every Las Vegas casino felt necessary to employ. In contrast to the usual hotel detectives, the security detail cared nothing for what went on in the bedrooms. A man might cheat on his wife, steal the linen or default on his bill, all with relative impunity—as long as he played honestly at the gambling tables.

A telephone call to the security office settled Bronko's current status speedily. No, Mr. Shaman was no longer employed by the Xanadu. No, they did not know Mr. Shaman's present whereabouts. However, if Mr. Duffy would care to speak with the present chief of security . . .

Mr. Duffy spoke instead to the bell captain. If the security detail could be said to be the hotel's FBI, then certainly the bellhops were its CIA, a depository of secrets, official and otherwise. Unlike the CIA, they were not adverse to sharing their intelligence for a price.

"Sure, I know Bronko," the bell captain admitted, pocketing Duffy's ten dollars with the skill of a frog swallowing a fly. "He a friend of yours?"

"You might say that."

"I wouldn't. Bronko isn't very popular around here. He got himself fired for skimming." The practice of pocketing a portion of the gambling take somewhere between the tables and the bank was a common—and illegal—stratagem used by some of the casinos to avoid taxes. But only by the management; it frowned on the help going into business for themselves.

Knowing the punishment that often followed such transgressions, Duffy asked, "Where should I look for him—the bottom of Lake Mead?"

"Naw. Bronko got off with a slap on the wrist. Kinda surprising, 'cause if there's one thing Mr. Loud doesn't dig, it's somebody else's hand in his pocket. Could be Bronko paid off the right guy to keep it quiet."

"Any idea where he went from here?"

"The rumor is he found himself a ranch someplace. Me, I don't buy it. Farmer was a dirty word to Bronko—like sucker. But maybe farming and ranching ain't the same thing." He eyed Duffy curiously. "You're a cop, aren't you? Not local or state, either—I know those mothers. That leaves federal. What's Uncle want Bronko for?"

"Would you believe burning his draft card?"

"Hell, I could care less. Bronko never did me no favors. But if I did want to find him, I'd maybe ask that broad of his. That is, if I could remember her name." He waited expectantly.

Duffy placed another ten dollar bill in his hand. "Mindy Queen," the bell captain exclaimed, his memory miraculously restored. He pointed to the placard on the lobby wall which advertised the current attractions in the theater-restaurant. Mindy Queen's name headed the list of the Kubla Kuties. "How about that! Been a snake, it'd have bitten me, right?"

Queen, M., was listed in the telephone directory. Her apartment was several miles from the Xanadu in distance and several light-years in expense.

She was just arising when Duffy rang her bell, although it was the middle of the afternoon. Her day began at nine, but that was P.M., not A.M. The filmy peignoir in which she greeted him was considerably less revealing than her working clothes. Mindy Queen was, in Las Vegas parlance, a show girl, a wholly apt description. She did not sing, dance, tell jokes or play a musical instrument. Her job required merely that she stand upon the stage or walk about it, looking beautiful, and for this Mindy was amply endowed. Her blonde hair was probably as false as the name she used, but her tall body was genuine and as lushly sensual as the ornate gold headboard and lavender sheets which Duffy could glimpse through the open doorway to her bedroom.

She admitted him without apprehension at the mention of Bronko's name. Men were no strangers to Mindy or to her apartment; she had long since ceased to worry about what the neighbors might think.

"I was just about to have a drink," she informed him with a yawn. "Want to join me?"

The Scotch was Glenlivet; when he complimented her taste, Mindy shrugged. "Bronko bought it. He goes for the best in everything."

"Same old Bronko. Hasn't changed a bit."

"Meaner, maybe." She added quickly. "Just kidding, of course. Where'd you know him from? I haven't seen you around here before."

"We did a little soldiering together once."

"Oh, you're one of them. Kind of late, aren't you?"

"I got here as soon as I could," he parried. "Have I missed something?"

"Well, I mean, the reunion or whatever was last month."

"Really? Well, maybe I can still make it. Where's it being held?"

"Didn't Bronko tell you?" Mindy regarded him with sudden suspicion. "Who you trying to con, mister? You weren't in the Army with Bronko. You're too young. You better get out of here."

Duffy sighed. "All right, I confess. I've never even met Bronko. Truth is, I'm researching a book on the Do Binh affair. I thought Bronko might help me out by telling his side of the story."

"I wouldn't know anything about that." Yet the lie reassured her somewhat. "A writer, huh? How come you didn't say so in the first place?"

"Gun-shy, I guess. The last guy I asked about Bronko jumped to the conclusion that I was from the FBI. Can you believe that?"

Mindy tittered. "You a G-man? With all that hair?"

"Right on. So if you'll tell me how to get in touch with Bronko—"

The merriment left her face. "I don't know where he is."

"You mentioned some sort of reunion."

"Did I? Okay, maybe I did. But I don't know anything about it. Not who, not why and not where, understand?"

Duffy understood. Mindy was plainly terrified of her lover; if she did possess the information he sought, she had no intention of divulging it. "I guess I'll just have to keep looking, then. Thanks for the drink. Maybe you'll let me return the favor—after the show tonight, for instance?"

"Well . . . I'm through about two-thirty. You could wait for me in the lounge."

"Now you're talking!" He meant it, although not in the way Mindy assumed. Her ready acceptance of the invitation proved what he already suspected, that Bronko Shaman—wherever he might be—was not in Las Vegas or close enough to be apprised that his mistress was dating another man.

Mindy followed him to the door. "Say, have you ever thought about doing a book about a show girl? I've seen things you wouldn't believe, the kind of dirt the public really digs. We could—what do they call it?—collaborate. I mean, all you'd have to do is write down what I tell you and we'd split the dough. We could make a fortune."

"I'll think it over." Duffy gave her a parting wink. "I

don't know how much money we'd make—but the fringe benefits sound great."

Mindy Queen would have to find another to write her exposé of backstage life—and to buy her a drink, for that matter. Duffy checked out of the Xanadu, pausing only long enough to dispatch a telegram to F.X. Raymond. While waiting in the terminal for his flight to depart, it occurred to him that he was one of the few tourists ever to leave Las Vegas without gambling. He put a quarter in a slot machine, his contribution to the economy. The machine returned him a profit of seventy-five cents—which seemed to sum up his visit: He had not hit the jackpot, but he had made enough to keep playing.

In Los Angeles he chose more modest accommodations, not in tardy deference to his expense account, but because he wished a central location. The following morning he was able to walk to the FBI's district office. The agent-in-charge, a hard-bitten veteran named Paul Collins, was not surprised to see him. Warning of Duffy's visit had preceded him via a lengthy teletype from Raymond slugged Hold for Arrival. Neither was Collins especially overjoyed. Special Assignments Detail operated somewhat outside the normal Bureau structure. Its members had on occasion been used to investigate practices and procedures within the Bureau itself. Hence, they were viewed with a wariness verging upon hostility.

Collins wasn't made happier by learning what Duffy required of him. "Do you know how big this city is? Twenty-five hundred square miles, that's how big. Do you know how many people there are in those twenty-five hundred square miles! Nearly five million! And you expect me to put the finger on two of them?"

"Relax, Paul. It's just simple legwork. At least, that's

what X-Ray told me."

"I don't have enough men to handle the cases we're already working on," Collins protested, the prelude to surrender. "Okay, go over it again."

"Heaston and Shaman arrived L.A. International on January 9 via Pan-Am from Mexico City. I'd like your office to survey the hotels for guests registering on that date. Not the fleabags, that ain't their style, just the good ones. See if you can find out where they stayed, for how long and next destination if given. At the same time I want all outgoing airline passenger manifests for the week following examined. Contact the car rental agencies to see if they leased an automobile, buzz Motor Vehicles in Sacramento in case they bought one. Public utilities should be able to tell you if they rented a house or took an apartment. Check the banks for new accounts opened in that time period." Duffy paused. "What am I forgetting?"

"How about the public library—in case they borrowed a book?"

"Oh, now I remember. The obvious one. Ask the police department if they're in jail."

"May I file a demurrer or two?" Collins asked caustically. "First, Heaston and Shaman may not be using their right names. Second, there are a half-dozen intrastate airlines operating out of L.A. International which don't file passenger manifests. Third, they may be staying with a friend."

"And, fourth, they're probably not in L.A., anyway. I agree with everything you say, Paul. Get your people on it right away, will you?"

"For two cents I'd squawk to Washington. Except I'm sure it wouldn't do me a damned bit of good. You could at least tell me what these two galoots have done that makes them worth my sweat."

"As far as I know, they haven't done a thing."

"And if you did know, you still wouldn't tell me, correct?"

"Those were my orders, Paul. Nothing personal."

"Yeah?" Collins replied skeptically. "Okay, where do I reach you—or is that another state secret?"

"Not at all. I'll be at the Statler, catching up on my beauty sleep."

Duffy returned to his hotel but not to sleep. He studied Raymond's teletype, reading it over and over until he had memorized the contents. The information he had requested was a rundown on the eleven men charged along with their commander and his first sergeant for the murder of the Vietnamese politician Do Binh. The summary, culled not only from the FBI files but from Internal Revenue, Social Security and Veterans Administration as well, sang a melancholy song. Three of the Hellions were dead, one by natural causes, a second in a barroom brawl, the third by his own hand. A fourth was as good as dead, confined by schizophrenia to a mental hospital. Of the survivors only one—Theodore Kitchen, attorney—could be said to have made something of himself since leaving the service. And of the five remaining, all had been in trouble with the law for offenses ranging from petty theft to manslaughter; two had served prison terms.

It was probably unfair to blame the trauma suffered in Vietnam for the sorry record. It could be argued just as plausibly that the men were natural misfits to begin with. In either case, Duffy had not been appointed to judge the past.

He had been appointed to investigate the present. Thus, two significant facts emerged from the teletype summary. Five of the former guerrillas—Guido Faccialorda, Richard Wald, Henry Plum, William Votaw, Leon Yocum—were listed as PWU: present whereabouts unknown. They had vanished from their usual haunts roughly coincident with Anthony Heaston's return to the United States. The sixth man—the attorney Kitchen—lived in Los Angeles, Anthony Heaston's port of entry.

Duffy would not have been surprised to learn that Ted Kitchen had also joined the ranks of the missing. However, a telephone call revealed that he was not only present but available.

Kitchen's law office was located in the Watts district. His practice was devoted to serving the interests of the black community of which he was a member. The tan stucco building was his home as well as his place of business; his wife doubled as his legal secretary. The modest surroundings were dictated by choice, not necessity, since the bar association rated his professional qualities highly.

Ted Kitchen was a lithe, handsome man of thirty-five with an Afro hair style. He wore a purple velvet blouse and tight-fitting striped trousers rather than the typical attorney's conservative business suit. "Mr. Duffy. I thought I knew all the local FBI, but your name is a new one."

"Let me hang an old one on you, Counselor. Anthony Heaston." He watched Kitchen's face.

It registered only surprise. "Anthony Heaston? Good Lord! Where is he?"

"I was hoping you could tell me that."

"Really? Why me?"

"You were a member of his outfit. Heaston's Hellions."

"Heaston's Hellions," Kitchen repeated softly. "Strange, how long ago that seems. PFC Ted Kitchen, 39022529. That's a lifetime away from Ted Kitchen, attorney-at-law. But one couldn't have happened without the other. Cause and effect. If it hadn't been for Colonel Heaston, I wouldn't be here."

"You mean he saved your life?"

"In a manner of speaking. I was a wild kid in those days, Mr. Duffy—hating the skin I had to live in and the world that wouldn't allow me to forget it. I joined Special Forces because I wanted to learn to kill. I learned how, all right. I also learned something else—that it was better to change the system than to destroy it. That's how Colonel Heaston saved my life. I'll always be grateful to him."

"Even though he got you a bad conduct discharge?"

"But that's just it, don't you see? I was given a closeup view of how justice works—or didn't work in that case. Before then it was all so damn mysterious, like God and death. The Do Binh affair showed me that justice is a human creation, not necessarily malevolent, but good or bad, depending on the men who mold it. When the Army kicked me out, I decided that I must become one of those men, hopefully on the side of good." Kitchen shrugged. "And here I am. Still hoping, incidentally."

"Tell me about Do Binh. What really happened?"

"President Carson called it a regrettable error," Kitchen parried. "Why not accept the official verdict? I have."

"How about the others?"

"I can't speak for the others. I never saw any of them again."

"The survivors are holding a reunion right now. I'm surprised you didn't get an invitation."

"I recognize an innuendo when I hear it, Mr. Duffy. You're suggesting that I did get an invitation and won't admit it."

"Heaston was in L.A. a few weeks ago. Since he contacted all the others, it strikes me as odd that he didn't at least give you a call."

"There were thirteen men charged in the Do Binh case. Someone pointed out the parallel and it haunted me for years. There were thirteen at the Last Supper also, Christ and His twelve disciples, one of whom betrayed Him." Kitchen nodded slowly. "Yes, I was the Judas. I betrayed Colonel Heaston. Not for thirty pieces of silver, but for a bottle of rotgut furnished by a reporter I thought was a buddy."

"Is that how you actually see it?" Duffy asked curiously. "Heaston as Christ, you as Iscariot?"

"I did at the time. I've come to understand myself better since. I wasn't really a traitor, just a posturing child who couldn't hold his liquor. I've come to understand Colonel Heaston better, too. He wasn't God the way I saw him then, but a human being with a special kind of magic, yet flawed like all human beings." He added, "The colonel forgave me for spilling my guts to the reporter. However, I don't really consider it strange that I wasn't invited to the reunion. Do you?"

"Sorry. I didn't mean to open an old wound."

"Why is the FBI interested in Colonel Heaston at this late date? I know, I know. It's just a routine investigation."

"You've been open with me, so I'll skip the usual baloney. I was ordered to locate Heaston and report on his activities. I don't really know why. I'm not sure anybody else does, either."

"Then you're not intending to arrest him? You'd swear to that?"

"Absolutely." Duffy studied his troubled expression. "Does that make a difference?"

"You can understand that I'm the last man in the world who would want to cause the Colonel more trouble. On the other hand, I am also an officer of the court." Kitchen hesitated. "You assumed that Colonel Heaston came to town to see me. Did you know that his wife—his ex-wife, that is—lives in Los Angeles, too?"

It wasn't entirely accurate; Evelyn Heaston, now Mrs. Norman Michaels, made her home in one of the score of smaller political entities which, together with the city proper, comprises the megalopolis called Los Angeles. Sherman Oaks lay across the mountains at the western end of the San Fernando Valley yet easily reached via two freeways, an attractive bedroom community for the upper middle class which generally worked elsewhere.

Following her divorce, the ex-Mrs. Heaston had worked for a time as a decorator for the May Company. There she met Michaels, a buyer for the same chain. She gained not only a husband but a family, since Michaels, a widower, had two teen-age children. Both were grown now, leaving Evelyn, without children of her own, to play bridge and golf, participate in charity work and run a house that was too big for two people.

This much Duffy knew from a cursory investigation. What he did not know, and was curious to learn, was whether Evelyn Michaels had recently resumed her relationship, innocent or otherwise, with her former husband.

There were a number of automobiles parked in the curving driveway of the ranch-style dwelling. None belonged to Anthony Heaston, however, or to Mr. and Mrs. Norman Michaels, according to the registrations. The lady of the house answered the door herself, since servants were beyond the reach of even the well-to-do these days. She was a tanned well-groomed woman, a trifle plump but still attractive. Duffy recognized that she had once been a beauty.

"FBI?" she repeated, her polite smile changing to bewilderment. "Goodness me! I'm sorry. My husband is out of town."

"It's you I came to see, Mrs. Michaels. May I come in?"

She admitted him with only momentary hesitation. "I'm entertaining my bridge club—"

"I'll get right to the point. I'm trying to locate Colonel Anthony Heaston. I hoped you might be able to tell me where he is."

"Tony?" Evelyn's eyes widened with astonishment. "How on earth would I know?"

"Colonel Heaston was in L.A. last month. I thought he might have gotten in touch with you."

"I had absolutely no idea."

Another hope blasted; Duffy sighed. "Well, if you should hear from the Colonel, I'd appreciate your letting us know."

"Why should I?" she asked with a hostility which surprised him. "Aren't you people ever going to quit? Haven't you persecuted him enough?"

"Perhaps I didn't make myself clear. It's just a routine—"

"You're a liar! If you're after Tony, it's simply to pick up where you left off years ago." She cut off his objection; he had tapped a well of bitterness that gushed forth in a torrent. "Don't try to fool me. I was there! I saw it happen! I know who's behind this. That evil old man—yes, I mean Orrin Kell Carson!—to blacken a man's reputation and not even allow him to defend himself. To take the finest soldier in the Army and put him to counting paper clips and training pigeons! And even that wasn't humiliating enough—they actually had the gall to pick Tony, of all men in the world, to draw up the plans for—for—" Evelyn ran out of breath if not indignation.

There was no reason to debate the matter, yet her vehemence made him curious. "If you felt such a loyalty to Colonel Heaston, why did you divorce him?"

"What makes you think I did?" she replied quietly. "The divorce was his idea, not mine. I would have stuck with him till hell froze over. But Tony knew what his future was going to be and that there was no way for me to be part of it. He was right, of course."

Of course; the existence of a mercenary guerrilla was nothing to offer to a woman. However, Duffy suspected that she would have been glad to share its hardships and its dangers—and perhaps would be, even yet. But since Heaston had chosen to follow his star without her, it seemed unlikely that he had changed his mind after all these years. "Please forgive me for bothering you, Mrs. Michaels. I hope I haven't spoiled your party."

"It's only a bridge game," Evelyn said with a shrug which summed up the barrenness of her existence. "There'll always be another."

Riding back in the taxi, Duffy reflected that, whatever the truth and whoever the villain, the Do Binh affair had claimed far more than one victim. Nor could he be sure that the casualty list was yet complete; the echoes of the shot which had killed the Vietnamese politician were still reverberating. When, if ever, would they finally stop?

Paul Collins had telephoned the hotel in his absence. Duffy returned the call. "We've struck pay dirt," Collins informed him with satisfaction not only for the success of his assignment but for the ease with which it had been accomplished. "Your men rented a car at the airport the day they hit L.A. They turned it in two days later in El Centro. That's down south in the Imperial Valley."

"And?"

"What do you mean—and? You asked us to find out where they went from here. Okay, we found out." What use Duffy put the information to didn't concern the FBI's agent-in-charge; Heaston and Shaman had removed themselves from his jurisdiction. However, he was willing to throw in an opinion. "My guess is that your two birds are probably in Mexico. El Centro's only a skip and a jump from the border."

Duffy was unable to accept the theory. If Mexico was Anthony Heaston's destination, why had he left it in the first place? "Give me the poop on the Imperial Valley, Paul. I've never been there."

"Flat and dry and hot. Marvelous soil, though. Most of the people are farmers."

"Farmers—or ranchers?"

"Farmers, ranchers, what's the difference?"

None as far as Duffy was concerned. On the other hand, Bronko Shaman might think there was all the difference in the world.

Juan Pedro Olvera was a Mexican by heritage, a Californian by birth and an El Centroan by choice. He was also, through longevity, the leading authority on the Imperial Valley's past and the generally accepted oracle on its future. Former president of the realty board, the chamber of commerce and a dozen other civic organizations, Olvera was a storehouse of information, ranging from last year's postal receipts to this year's tomato crop. Though past seventy, he still operated his own office—and piloted his own plane.

Olvera was delighted to be able to expound (some might call it brag) on the virtues of his beloved Valley, particularly to a representative of out-of-state interests with money to invest. And to conduct him on an aerial survey of the area. Duffy learned that the one-time delta of the Colorado —provided with rich soil by the river, blessed with year-round sunshine by geography, supplied with water by man through an eighty-mile network of canals—ranked fourth among U.S. counties in agricultural production. No less than twenty different crops earned over a million dollars annually; cattle, lettuce and cotton were the most profitable.

There were actually two valleys, easily distinguishable from each other by their colors. One was green, the vast farmland embraced by the canals. The second was the gray-brown desert where, with only the meager rainfall to sustain it, little flourished save cactus and mesquite.

"One of these days we'll irrigate the Yuha, too," Olvera boasted, indicating the barren waste that stretched west to the lavender-hued mountains. "But that's years off and you're interested in the *aqui y ahora,* the here and now. I'm assuming it's tillable land you're looking for."

"At the moment, I'm looking at everything."

"Well, I can tell you what's available in two words. Not much. There's precious little turnover in farmland these days. What is for sale is priced 'way too high, at least in my opinion. Course, if you were buying for the future, there's plenty of acreage in the Yuha that can be snapped up for a song." He added, "I'm not advising it, understand. Not unless you figured to put in a resort like those hombres over Pinto way—and I don't think much of that idea, either."

Duffy, who until now had garnered little but statistics from the flight, felt a prickle of interest. "What kind of a resort?"

"*Quién sabe?* A bunch took over the old Tres Muertos ranch about the first of January. Used to be a movie location, you know, westerns and that kind of thing. Been vacant for years. Don't know who the new owners are. The transaction wasn't handled locally."

"You've made me curious. Would it be too much trouble to fly over that way?"

"No trouble at all. I'm a little curious myself." Olvera

turned the aircraft south toward Signal Mountain, the solitary peak which reared out of the desert floor on the Mexican side of the border, then west along the international boundary. "Hard to believe the whole Valley looked like that less than a hundred years ago," he said disparagingly of the parched and desolate landscape below. "Good for nothing except snakes and jackrabbits. *Agua, dinero y sudor* made the difference, Mr. Duffy. Water, money and sweat. Anyone tackling the Yuha better have plenty of all three." He pointed ahead. "Tres Muertos is on the other side of those hills."

"Is that its fence?"

Olvera regarded the chain-link barrier, still new enough to reflect the late afternoon sunlight, with surprise. "Must be. I hadn't seen it before." He added grudgingly, "Guess the new owners have the money. Maybe the sweat, too. But I guarantee they don't have the water."

The fence fell behind them. They swooped low over the eroded foothills and into the shallow valley beyond. The buildings clustered there resembled a tiny village, a dozen houses arranged along a wide unpaved street. But it was not actually a village; most of the structures were mere façades, intended to deceive the camera. Only the largest appeared to be inhabitable, and was inhabited, to judge by the smoke curling up from its chimney and the two automobiles parked beside it.

"Would you look at that!" Olvera indicated a salmon-pink helicopter that stood a short distance west of the village. The ungainly bird, a civilian version of the Army's UH-1D Huey troop carrier, roosted on a nest of sunbaked earth, its long rotor blades drooping like bedraggled feathers. "What do you suppose they need that for?"

Duffy was staring at a discovery of his own. At the far end of the street was a ramshackle representation of a railroad station from a bygone era. Drawn up alongside its sagging platform was a train of equally ancient vintage. The bulky steam engine with its coal tender was the type seldom seen these days outside railroad museums. The baggage car, two coaches and caboose could have been fugitives from the same museum.

"Left over from the last movie they made there," his pilot explained. "Doubt if it runs any more. Wouldn't get you anyplace even if it did." The tracks, although stretching east and west from the station, eventually curved to meet and form a circle several miles in diameter like a giant version of a child's toy train set.

Olvera banked the aircraft around to permit a second flyover. This time they not only saw but were seen. Several men, alerted by the engine overhead, appeared on the porch of the large building. They stared but did not wave as the plane passed above them. Duffy was unable to recognize any of the upturned faces. He was able to count them. Five out of a possible seven . . . if indeed these were the remnants of Heaston's Hellions.

"Seen enough?" Olvera put the plane on a northeasterly heading without waiting for an answer. "Well, it would appear those hombres mean business. They may even be able to turn the old place into a resort, at that."

Duffy nodded although his agreement was only partial. The men at Tres Muertos might mean business, all right. But he found it difficult to believe that it would turn out to be the resort business.

A title search disclosed that the ranch's last owner of record was Forte Enterprises, Inc. Forte was an example of that modern phenomenon, the conglomerate, gathering beneath its corporate umbrella a number of diversified firms, not necessarily homogenous. Land development was only one of its activities; others ran the gamut from electronics and pharmaceuticals to pet food and parking lots. Forte's management was as sprawling as its interests. It was chartered by Delaware, its board of directors met in Chicago, but its main office was located in Beverly Hills.

Duffy succeeded in obtaining an appointment with Forte's executive vice-president, Ira Niblo. Not without difficulty, however; he overcame the attempts of three secretaries to fob him off on a subordinate and, failing that, to ascertain his business. Experience had taught him to deal with the top man wherever possible. Underlings usually did not possess the knowledge he sought or were reluctant to reveal it if they did.

He arrived at the Wilshire Boulevard address punctually. A receptionist directed him via express elevator to the executive level atop the building; junior officers and clerical personnel occupied the floor beneath. Here he was scrutinized by a second receptionist, who verified his appointment before permitting him to advance farther.

Delicately etched glass doors separated this smaller lobby from the offices beyond. Duffy reached them at the same moment as a woman approaching from the other side. She was a handsome creature, nearly as tall as he but younger; he guessed late twenties. Her slender body was concealed from throat to ankle by a peach-colored pants suit, not an unusual costume for Southern California. However, her fine-boned rather imperious face wore no make-up—which was unusual—and her long chestnut hair was gathered into a not too becoming bun.

Duffy lengthened his stride in order to open the door for her. The woman didn't appear to notice the courtesy—or him; she swept by without a glance. "You're welcome, I'm sure," he murmured.

The young woman was aware of him, after all. She

wheeled about. "For your information," she said in a voice as cold as her gaze was hot, "I am perfectly capable of opening doors for myself. And, furthermore, I prefer to."

"Excuse me, sir. I mistook you for a lady."

The blue eyes measured him scornfully, then their owner resumed her march to the elevator. She did not look back but jabbed repeatedly at the demand button like a swordsman skewering a foe. He wondered what had made her so angry—not him, certainly—or whether she was simply abrasive by nature. If so, it seemed a shame; she was a striking woman otherwise.

His next encounter with the opposite sex was more pleasant. Ira Niblo's private secretary, Pamela Frain, was nearly as attractive and considerably less hostile. Her diminutive voluptuous figure seemed lost behind the huge desk. She had to stand to search through the papers that littered it in order to find her appointment calendar. "You'll have to forgive me," she explained. "Mr. Niblo's regular secretary is in the hospital and I'm just filling in for her. I still haven't gotten the hang of it." If the job was strange to her, men were not; a coquettish smile accompanied the apology, while one hand arranged the red hair on which ample effort had already been expended. "Oh, here we are. Mr. Duffy, eleven o'clock. You're right on time. Mr. Niblo isn't, though."

The coffee table held an assortment of reading material but not the type usually found in a waiting room. The book Duffy picked up was Sandburg's biography of Abraham Lincoln. The magazines beside it were published by a historical society devoted to the same subject. "Who's the Lincoln scholar, Miss Frain? Not you, certainly."

"Why not me?"

"For one thing, you're not the regular girl. For another—"

"I know. I'm more the *McCall's* type. You're so right. They belong to Mr. Niblo. He's really hung on the subject. There's even an article by him in one of those magazines, the November issue, in case you're interested."

"I'm the *Playboy* type myself."

"Sorry about that. Around here it's Honest Abe or nothing."

"Then is it okay if I just admire the beautiful scenery?"

Pamela acknowledged the flattery with an exaggerated flutter of lashes. "That's what scenery's for, isn't it?" She busied herself with the papers on the desk, conscious of his gaze but not at all flustered by it. An occasional flirtation was a fringe benefit every young secretary had the right to expect.

The telephone buzzed before either tired of the game. Pamela told Duffy, a shade regretfully, "You may go in now."

The room he entered bore more resemblance to a museum than the private office of a corporation vice-president. A bookcase crammed to overflowing with volumes on Niblo's hobby filled one wall. Framed letters and handwritten documents on the same subject (which Duffy took to be originals) occupied another, while a bronze bust of the sixteenth President stood in a corner. Even the desk appeared old enough to have been his property.

The man who rose from behind it to greet him did not seem out of place in these surroundings. At first glance, Ira Niblo bore a resemblance to the Great Emancipator, a tall gaunt man with sunken eyes and a deeply cleft chin. However, his hair was silver not black, his cheeks beardless and his slightly sibilant voice carried no trace of a midwestern twang.

He offered Duffy a chair and an apology. "I seem to be chronically behind schedule. I start each day with good intentions. By noon it's the same old shambles." And, indeed, he wore the harried expression of one to whom twenty-four hours per day were not enough. His manner betrayed an insecurity which Duffy had noted in other men with too much responsibility and not quite enough authority. He gave the impression of constantly glancing over his shoulder as if expecting a reprimand.

"Don't mention it. Your waiting room's quite fascinating."

"You're interested in Lincoln?" Niblo inquired, his eyes brightening. Then he chuckled. "No, I imagine you're referring to Miss Frain. At your age I found a live girl much more rewarding than a dead President myself."

"I understand you're an authority on the subject. Dead Presidents, that is."

"Only one. Around here the joke—which I'm not supposed to have heard—is that I won't be satisfied until someone assassinates me. Well, Mr. Duffy, how can I serve you?"

"I represent Eastern interests which I am not at liberty to identify just yet. My principals are exploring the possibility of obtaining the mineral rights to certain property in the southwestern portion of the Imperial Valley. Among the parcels they're interested in is one called the Tres Muertos ranch, which I discover is owned by Forte Enterprises."

"It is?" Niblo asked blankly. "I don't mind revealing my ignorance. Frankly, it's quite beyond me to stay current on every last item in our inventory. Anyway, why should I —when I have others to do it for me?" He picked up the telephone and said, "Miss Frain, put me through to Mr. Sullivan. Fred, Ira Niblo. I've had an inquiry regarding the availability of the Tres Muertos ranch—no, Tres, T-r-e-s—in the Imperial Valley. What can you tell me about it?" He listened, thanked his informant and hung up. "Tres Muertos was leased last November. I'm afraid you're a trifle late."

"That's too bad."

"Indeed it is," Niblo agreed regretfully. "The rental is shockingly low. But the property had been lying fallow for several years so we took what we could get."

He was interrupted by the appearance of Pamela Frain at the door. "Telephone call, Mr. Niblo!" Her excitement seemed excessive for the routine announcement. "Overseas operator!"

Niblo reacted in the same fashion. "Put it right through! Mr. Duffy, if you'll excuse me—"

"I'll wait outside." He still had a question or two which Niblo might answer. Who had signed the lease for the ranch, for example? As he left the office, Forte's executive vice-president was on his feet, facing the telephone as if in the presence of royalty.

"Oh, how I'd love to listen in," Pamela murmured, more to herself than to Duffy. "But it'd mean my head if they found out. It might almost be worth it, though."

"Don't. It's a very pretty head."

He gained only an absent smile; her thoughts were on the conversation she could imagine but not hear. "I wouldn't bother waiting if I were you."

"My interview wasn't over."

"That's what you think. When the big boss phones, Mr. Niblo runs. Either to the airport to catch a plane, or to the nearest bar to grab a drink. You won't see him again today whichever and neither will I." She sighed. "It must be tough, a man his age, to have to take what he takes—and not even get paid a decent salary. Though I guess no salary would be really enough."

"Mind if I hang around, anyway? You may be wrong."

The phone buzzed; Pamela snatched it up. "Yes, sir. The one P.M. flight. I'll arrange for the visa. Your passport will be waiting for you at the airport. Have a good trip, Mr. Niblo." She replaced the receiver with a triumphant smile. "Switzerland. You lose, Mr. Duffy."

"Not necessarily. I still have you. I can't offer you Switzerland, but I can buy you lunch."

Eight-thirty Los Angeles time is equivalent to eleven-thirty in Washington, D.C. Duffy's pre-breakfast telephone call the next morning caught Raymond preparing to go to lunch. "You bet I remember you," Raymond told him. "George Upp won't let me forget because O.K. won't let him. I hope you've been working hard."

"Night and day," Duffy said, secure in the knowledge that Raymond could not see him stretched out in the queen size bed, the telephone perched on his bare chest. "I've found your missing colonel. He and Shaman and a few others are holed up on a ranch in the Imperial Valley desert doing business as the HH Company, which I interpret to stand for Heaston's Hellions."

"What kind of business?"

"Depends on which story you want to believe. According to Shaman's girl friend, they're holding a reunion of the old outfit. According to Forte Enterprises, which owns the land they're leasing, the HH Company intends to build a resort, sort of a dude ranch."

"H'm," said Raymond dubiously. "Which do you believe, Jake?"

"Neither. You don't form a company and lease a ranch at the end of nowhere to hold a reunion. And you don't spring a man out of prison and round up a bunch of misfits to build a resort. Add to this the fact that the HH Company has put up an expensive fence, bought a helicopter and God knows what else—all of which costs money none of them have. So there must be another reason, but what it is I can't even guess."

"Guesses don't make it, anyway. We've got to know. You figure out some clever way to get behind that fence without arousing suspicion. You say it's desert country? Maybe you could pose as a prospector or a Mexican wetback—"

"No thanks, F.X. I got eyes for going first class."

Duffy was replacing the receiver when Pamela Frain came in from the bathroom. Her body was swathed in a huge towel and her red hair curled in damp ringlets. "Shower's all yours, sweetie." She seated herself at the dressing table. "Who were you talking to?"

"My firm back East. Don't worry, I reversed the charges. I wouldn't stick a lady with a huge phone bill. Other things, maybe."

"It's not that huge, so quit bragging. Come here and powder my back. Ye gods, look at the time! I'm going to be late to work."

"Call in sick. You don't have anything to do with Niblo gone, anyhow."

"Get thee behind me. You already seduced me into taking yesterday afternoon off. If I don't punch in today . . . You're a bad influence, lover. A girl could get into a lot of trouble listening to you."

"Trouble? Last night you called it fun." He kissed the nape of her neck. "How quick they forget!"

Pamela turned on the bench to permit his lips to reach a more customary target. "Have it your way. It was fun. The strange thing is I thought at first that all you were really interested in was pumping me about that old ranch."

She was right, of course. He had cultivated Niblo's secretary for the information denied him by Niblo's hasty departure. However, business and pleasure are not always mutually exclusive and Duffy didn't mind mixing them when practical. He felt no qualm of conscience. Pamela had enjoyed the game as much as he; neither invested it with any real significance.

Now the game was over and both knew it. Pamela made a token gesture toward extending it. "I do have to dash, Jake. But take my phone number and if you're free this evening—"

"I'll take your number, but I'm shoving off this afternoon. Since you refuse to share my last day in town, I guess I'll have to kill the lonely hours by taking in a movie or something."

Anthony Heaston sat cross-legged on top of a knoll, the morning sun warming his back, while he studied the terrain below with the practiced gaze of the guerrilla. The narrow wash to his left, carved by countless flash floods, offered concealment for a platoon or more, an ideal spot to ambush a column moving on the road beyond with mortar fire from the knoll to cover the retreat. In his imagination he visualized the swift savage skirmish, the explosion of the land mines beneath the first vehicles, the pop-pop-pop of automatic weapons as they cut down the survivors . . . It was only a mental exercise, since in this vast desert there existed not one enemy to ambush, but it was an exercise which Heaston found stimulating.

Below him, the work party was engaged in another sort of exercise far less enjoyable. Stripped to the waist, they labored to chop the mesquite and greasewood and to stack the branches into piles. Now and then a rabbit or a ground squirrel, its lair threatened, darted away through the brush in panic and above a fringe-winged turkey vulture circled curiously. The five men, neither predators nor prey, paid no attention to these lesser inhabitants of the wasteland.

Bronko Shaman trudged up the slope to where Heaston sat. His broad face and barrel chest were coated with dust etched by numerous rivulets of sweat. "Take a break!" he bellowed. The work party straightened up gratefully and, stretching to relieve cramped muscles, sauntered toward the jeep which held the canteens of water.

Bronko tossed his machete to the earth and followed it with his body. "Damn stoop labor. And when I think how fast that frigging wood burns—"

"The wood's only half of it. The other half is the conditioning. They were in pretty sad shape when they checked in here."

"Well, what could you expect? Been a long time, Colonel. None of us is exactly the man he used to be. Except me and thee."

"Thee, maybe. Me—well, I'll be fifty years old next month and there are days when it seems closer to a hundred."

"You haven't changed one bit since Nam," Bronko scoffed. "Everybody says so."

"Everybody's wrong," Heaston said moodily. "Just between us, that stretch in La Tumba came mighty close to finishing me. First time in my life that I really felt licked. It wasn't only being caged up, though that was bad enough, God knows. The worst part was knowing that, barring a miracle, I was going to die right there in that stinking prison."

Introspection was foreign to Bronko's pragmatic nature; he could not share or understand the other man's terror. "Dying's dying. I don't much care where or how as long as it ain't soon."

Heaston plucked a weed and studied it somberly. "I disagree. I've lived closer to death than most. I believe I can say honestly that I'm not afraid of it. All I ask is that when

I go, it's with flags flying and bugles blowing—not be thrown out with the garbage."

"What are we talking about it for, anyway?" Bronko said uneasily. "We still got a lot of living to do, Colonel. And the best is yet to come. Not getting cold feet, are you?"

"Call it pregame butterflies. I never did enjoy sweating out the kickoff."

"The word'll be coming through soon enough. If you've got to worry about something"—Bronko spoke in the slightly patronizing manner of one who considered worry a weakness—"worry about how you're going to spend that million bucks."

"I haven't thought that far ahead. Have you?"

"I figure to buy me an island someplace, stock it shore-to-shore with strong booze and weak women and see which gives out first—me or the million."

"I'll wish you a dead heat." But when pressed for his own dream, Heaston shook his head. "I haven't formulated any plans for afterward. Or for the million, if I ever get it. To be truthful, the money doesn't really matter to me. I'm in this for something else."

"Sure. And you'll get that, all right. We all will. But if you was to give me the choice between that and the million . . . I crave the soft life and I've never quite been able to afford it." He added slyly, "Not having been an officer, you see."

Heaston cuffed him affectionately. "Don't be such a damn snob. You were the best topkick in the Army. That's better than being an officer any day. Hell, there were times when I almost thought you were running the old outfit instead of me. The men felt closer to you, and that's a fact."

Bronko accepted the compliment with a shrug. "Only natural. I wore stripes and you wore eagles. But you called the shots, then as now."

"I hope I can call them better now than I did then."

"Live and learn, I always say." Recognizing the return of the melancholia which disturbed him, Bronko changed the subject. "By the way, been meaning to tell you. Guido checked in El Centro on that plane that buzzed us the other day. Belongs to an old coot named Olvera, a real estate man. He uses it to show his customers around the Valley. So I guess it wasn't a snooper, after all."

"That makes me even happier that I didn't let Hack take a shot at it, the way he wanted. We'd have had the law out here on the double, asking questions I'd rather not answer. Let's remember that we're on this ranch legitimately and we've got the paper to prove it. Make certain everybody understands that. Hack especially.

"Don't worry about Hack. He's not too strong in the brains department, but he'll do what I tell him."

"Hack's trigger-happy. That could be a problem."

"Well, you've got to remember what happened to him. Napalmed by our own people, thinking he was VC. He's had a—what d'you call it?—a phobia about airplanes ever since."

"Hack's not the only one with that phobia." Heaston smiled. "Fortunately for us, I might add."

Bronko looked puzzled. After a moment he smiled also as if tardily understanding a joke. "Yeah. You can say that again, Colonel."

The music swelled as "The End" appeared on the screen. Both words and music faded. The house lights came on and the momentary silence was broken by the clapping of a single pair of hands. Their owner turned to the man slouched in the next loge seat; together, they composed the entire audience in the small projection room.

"Hell of a fine job, Shelly."

Sheldon Spydell yawned. "Where were you when we needed you, Jake?" He was a short plump man approximately the same age as Duffy, although the receding hairline made him appear older. The hornrim glasses imparted an owlish look to the round face. He and Duffy were not only friends but relatives; their mothers had been sisters. They were better friends now than as boys. The Feldmans were Orthodox Jews; they had never forgiven their daughter's ill-fated marriage outside her faith or completely accepted her mongrel son. Sheldon Spydell had long since shed the prejudices of childhood. Following the success of his first novel, he had come to Hollywood to earn more money, if less recognition, as a screenwriter. *The Thunder and the Sun,* the picture they had just viewed, was his last feature assignment. Spydell was now creator and executive producer of a TV adventure series currently in its fourth season.

"You say the picture was a flop? How come? I always heard that westerns were sure-fire box office."

"Nevertheless, a bomb. A torpedo is more like it. You've seen the film that sank a whole studio. Not to mention setting me adrift on the Sargasso Sea of TV."

"It cost too much? Was that the problem?"

"Not really. *The Thunder and the Sun* was out of touch with the times. By which I mean there were no four-letter words, no rape, no fellatio, no cunnilingus, no homosexuals. All the humping took place off-screen and the only genitals you saw belonged to the horses. Worst of all, it actually showed justice and virtue emerging triumphant."

"Sorry if I revived bitter memories, Shelly."

"Doesn't matter, as long as you saw what you wanted to see. Did you?"

"I think so." Exteriors for the big western had been

filmed on the Tres Muertos location; indeed, it was the last film to shoot there. Since the exteriors comprised over seventy-five per cent of the finished film, Duffy was now as well acquainted with the ranch (or, at least, the ranch as it had existed six years previously) as if he had visited it personally. "Do I dare ask another favor?"

"Anything—as long as it isn't running the film again."

"I want to pay a visit to Tres Muertos and I need a cover. If you could fix me up with whatever it takes to look like a producer, I might claim to be scouting locations for my next movie."

"Hell, you're already half-Jewish. All you need is a script, and I've got a whole trunkful. I can even let you use a company car. You buy the gas, naturally. Speaking of gas, reminds me—you're invited to dinner."

"I'd love to come, but I've got to shove off this afternoon. I hope Selena will understand."

"She won't. She's already peeved at you. You know Selena, little mother to all the world. When I told her you were in town, her first words were 'So why isn't your cousin staying with us like always? He's too important already to associate with the family?'"

"Tell her next time for sure. Better yet, I'll phone her myself."

"Nize baby. She does adore you, Jake; why, I'll never understand. If you weren't such a confirmed bachelor, I'd be jealous."

"I'm not a confirmed anything. Your side of the family wouldn't allow it. Now if Selena only had a sister as sweet and sexy as she is . . ."

"Well, she does have a brother in Greenwich Village we're not too sure about."

"Thanks just the same. A fellow I can always get. All it takes is a requisition."

Duffy was at the El Centro airport to meet Neddie Zigonis when he arrived from Houston by way of Phoenix the next afternoon. Zigonis was a dapper young man, swarthy of face and slight of stature. His breezy personality and the valises he habitually carried gave the impression of a successful drummer, jet-age style. However, Zigonis was rated the Bureau's top O and S agent (for observation and surveillance, a euphemism for wire-tapping and other forms of eavesdropping). His valises contained, not manufacturer's samples but an elaborate assortment of electronic monitoring equipment.

A hot wind was gusting across the parking lot, creating tiny dust devils and pelting exposed skin with stinging gritty particles. "And I thought Houston was miserable!" Zigonis said sourly. "At least it's part of civilization. I hope the hotel has air-conditioning."

Duffy indicated the travel trailer attached to the Spydell Productions sedan. "It doesn't."

Zigonis groaned. "What sort of a caper is this, anyway?"

"Didn't X-Ray tell you?"

"All he said was that Duffy had gotten himself in over his head as usual and that I was supposed to bail you out as usual."

"That's roughly correct. I'll explain as we drive."

"I got a hunch I won't like it any better after I've heard it," Zigonis grumbled. "If I'd wanted to serve amid the burning sands, I'd have joined the Foreign Legion. My God! Do you suppose I did?"

They followed the freeway west toward the escarpment of the Laguna Mountains. At Ocotillo they swung south on the state highway to a road, graded but unpaved, which branched off into the broad valley where the Tres Muertos ranch was located. They encountered no other vehicles or signs of life save for an occasional lizard scampering across their path. However, an infrequent trailer similar to the one Duffy had rented in El Centro, parked amid the brush, proved that the desert was inhabited by other human beings, if only intermittently. The trailers, some of which appeared to have been stationed for years, served as weekend retreats for city dwellers who sought the sun or collected rocks, two commodities with which the Yuha was abundantly supplied. Many of the trailers had carports attached; a few boasted covered patios; nearly all sprouted television antennas.

Duffy halted their own trailer on a boulder-studded plateau within sight of the Tres Muertos' chain-link fence but not the pseudo-western town. "I estimate the distance at a shade over two miles. What do you think? We can't get much closer."

"It makes it, I guess." Zigonis surveyed the harsh surroundings with disfavor. "What's a nice Greek boy doing in a hellhole like this?"

The trailer, although compact, was nearly as self-sustaining as a space capsule; it could sleep four adequately and two comfortably. There was water for washing, propane for cooking, plus a gasoline-driven generator to provide electricity when outside power sources were unavailable. "Plenty of beer in the refrigerator and baklava in the pantry," Duffy informed his glum companion. "Why, after a day or two of all this luxury, they'll have to drag you away."

"Yeah, to the booby hatch. I never saw so much scenery in my life!"

There was, however, a certain charm to the desolation. Even Zigonis admitted it, although grudgingly. Both men were city-born and bred, familiar with its turmoil, calloused to its cacophony. Here there was neither. Beyond the reach of traffic and telephones, the pervading quality was silence. The only light other than their own came from the moon which painted the desert with eerie beauty. They breathed air untainted by smog and saw stars they had nearly forgotten existed.

Yet once during the night they were made aware that others shared the wilderness. Duffy was awakened by what he first took to be the sound of a low-flying airliner. Listening more intently, he recognized the distinctive clatter of a helicopter. The Huey did not approach their campsite. The noise faded away in the distance and did not return. Why are they flying at night? he wondered. He could think of no satisfactory explanation.

The following morning he set out to find it if he could. Unhitching the trailer, they took the Spydell Productions sedan and continued down the road toward Tres Muertos. Left behind were the valises crammed with monitoring devices; in their place Zigonis carried a bulging briefcase. Left behind also were the business suits that were virtually the Bureau's uniform. They wore sport clothes casual in style and gaudy in color.

"Mighty sharp cats," Zigonis observed, more pleased with his costume than anything heretofore. "I always had eyes for being a big movie producer."

"I'm the big producer," Duffy reminded him. "You're the not-so-big assistant. Your job is to say 'Yes, Mr. Duffy' and don't you forget it."

"Guess it's true what they say about Hollywood. Nothing but small talents and big egos."

They reached the chain-link fence and found their path blocked by a gate secured by a large padlock. Duffy went to work with a slender steel pick. As he expected, the lock yielded easily. "Anybody peeking?"

Zigonis pointed to a shape in the sky. "Could be that helicopter you mentioned. Matter of fact, it better be—

because if they breed birds that size in these parts, I'm getting the hell out of here."

Their invasion might be unexpected, but it did not go undetected. They were barely under way again when the helicopter came toward them like a hawk which has spotted its prey. It hovered for a moment above them but did not pounce, swinging away again to vanish behind the low hills. "Calling out the guard," Duffy guessed. His surmise was correct. Rounding a curve, they found the road blocked by a jeep. The two men it contained approached warily, their hands hovering near but not quite touching the butts of the .45 pistols holstered at their waists.

The bigger of the pair wore a scowl as his permanent expression. This, plus the thick neck and the dark auburn fuzz which covered his chest and arms and head, made him resemble a bad-natured gorilla. The smaller man might have been his trainer. He was lithe of body and graceful of movement and, though he was garbed identically to his companion, managed to wear the white skivvy shirt and blue jeans with a certain dash. Beneath the black curly hair lay an Italianate face whose full lips curved naturally into a smile. Duffy had seen neither before yet he knew both from their photographs. The scowler was Henry Plum, called Hack; the smiler was Guido Faccialorda. While he had not doubted that he would find Heaston's Hellions at Tres Muertos, the confirmation was satisfying.

He gave them both an ingratiating grin. "Hi, there. You folks live around these parts?"

"Damn right," Hack Plum growled. "This is private property, savvy?"

Guido put a hand on his arm. "Better hear what he has to say. Remember the Colonel's orders."

Since Hack appeared ready to argue the point, Duffy

took quick advantage of the opening. "My name is Duffy and this is my assistant, Mr. Zigonis. We work for Spydell Productions"—he tapped the gold lettering on the door for emphasis—"and we drove down from Hollywood to scout the ranch as the possible location for a film we're going to make. We certainly didn't mean to trespass. But when we found the gate unlocked—"

"He's lying, Guido. I locked the gate myself."

"Yeah. Except, come to think of it, I was the last one through. When I went into town a couple days ago. Anyway, it doesn't matter." He told Duffy, "Sorry. The ranch isn't available. You'll have to leave."

"Now wait a minute," Duffy protested with a show of indignation. "We've come a long way. The least you can do is to let us talk to your boss. He might be interested in my proposition."

Hack's scowl grew more ominous. Once again Guido intervened. "Maybe the man's got a point. Let's dump it in the Skipper's lap, okay?" He sauntered back to the jeep without waiting for agreement, leaving Hack to mount a sullen guard.

Duffy attempted to draw him into conversation. Failing, he began to chat with Zigonis regarding the splendor of their surroundings, meanwhile watching from the corner of his eye as Guido carried on a lengthy conversation via the jeep's shortwave radio with—Duffy felt sure—Anthony Heaston.

Guido returned with an I-told-you-so glance for Hack. "The Colonel says that being as how you've come this far you might as well come the rest of the way."

As they followed the jeep down the road, Zigonis murmured, "What would you have done if the answer had been no?"

"Gone ahead, anyway—after we'd taken their pistols, of

course."

"Where do you get that 'we' stuff? I'm no bloody hero type."

"Stick around, Neddie. You're about to meet one."

Three men awaited them on the broad shaded porch of the mock town's largest and only inhabitable building. Beneath the uncurtained windows of the upper story, a faded sign proclaimed it to be the Last Chance Saloon. Duffy recognized Anthony Heaston instantly. Even if he had not, he would have known instinctively that here was the group's leader from his bearing, the indefinable yet unmistakable aura of command.

Heaston, secure in his own authority, felt no need to stand on protocol. He came down the wooden steps with hand outstretched. "I'm Anthony Heaston. Welcome to Tres Muertos, Mr.—Duffy, is it?"

"Right on. And this is Mr. Zigonis, my associate." Duffy met the probing deep-set eyes with a smile. "You did say 'welcome,' didn't you? After the reception we got up the road—"

"I'm sorry about that. We've had some trouble with vandals the past month, and since we weren't expecting company . . ."

"That makes us even. I wasn't expecting to find anybody on the ranch. I supposed the old place was deserted. When your guards jumped us, I began to wonder if maybe we hadn't stumbled onto an atomic testing range."

Heaston smiled. "Nothing like that." He did not explain what it was like, however. Instead, he beckoned the other two men forward. "Let me introduce my associates. Mr. Shaman. Mr. Wald."

Although not as openly hostile as Hack Plum, neither shared their leader's cordiality. Bronko Shaman's thin lips murmured a greeting which the opaque stare contradicted;

he measured the strangers with cold skepticism. Richard Wald appeared more apprehensive than suspicious. Behind dark glasses, his eyes looked everywhere but at Duffy and Zigonis. Duffy understood why the Hellions called him Moby Dick. He resembled a small whale in shape and was an albino besides, with skin and hair the same sickly white. Moby Dick was twice the size of the squat Bronko yet, Duffy sensed, far less dangerous. He reminded himself that the estimate was relative; all had been trained in a savage school.

Heaston said, "I understand you're in the motion picture business. Will you forgive me if I confess that your name doesn't ring a bell?"

"We're still even. I never heard of you either, Mr. Heaston. Or should that be Colonel Heaston?"

"United States Army, retired. Very retired, actually. Were you in the service, Mr. Duffy?"

"My back kept me out. I've got a yellow streak running down the middle of it."

The hoary joke drew a giggle from Moby Dick; Bronko merely looked bored. Heaston said, "Oh, I doubt that. You strike me as a pretty gutty customer. Level with me. Was that gate really unlocked?"

Discretion demanded that he continue the fiction. But something in the other man challenged him to take up the gauntlet. "Not really. I fiddled with it until it opened." He sensed rather than saw Zigonis shudder. "After coming this far, damned if I was going to let a little lock stop me."

Audacity triumphed; Heaston roared with laughter. "I knew it! I don't often misjudge men. If you'd have said no, I'd have asked you to leave. Now I'm going to invite you to have lunch with us. Bronko, tell the cook to lay on a couple of extra places."

"Anything you say, Colonel," Bronko murmured, acknowledging the order but obviously not pleased by it. He wheeled about smartly and marched through the swinging doors of the saloon. Moby Dick, after a moment of hesitation, lumbered after him.

"I expect you'll want to wash up before chow, Mr. Duffy. And perhaps join me in a drink."

"Sounds great. Neddie, bring the briefcase. Colonel Heaston might like to take a look at our script before we talk business."

Heaston shook his head. "Perhaps Guido and Hack didn't make it clear, but Tres Muertos isn't available for filming just now."

"Bring it along, anyway," Duffy told Zigonis. "In case the Colonel changes his mind after hearing my pitch."

The big room had been constructed to fit Hollywood's conception of a frontier saloon and gambling hell which had probably never existed anywhere outside the cinema. The floor was stout planking, the massive bar which occupied most of one wall was carved mahogany and the paneled walls were embellished with nineteenth-century gingerbread. A broad staircase (for the inevitable free-for-all) ascended to a horseshoe-shaped interior balcony which gave access to a half-dozen bedrooms. Every saloon had its ladies of easy virtue, as any filmgoer could attest. However, the Last Chance was only a shell; the furnishings had long since been removed. Gone were the velvet drapes with their golden tassels and on the walls were rectangles, lighter in shade than the surrounding wood, which indicated where paintings had hung. Gone also was the mirror behind the bar (meant to be shattered by the obligatory bottle) as well as the round tables at which countless actors had pretended to slake their thirst and to gamble away their wages. What furniture there was had been placed there by the saloon's present tenants: a radio which blared rock music and a long harvest table with a covey of steel folding chairs.

The table was set for seven. The cook, under Bronko's supervision, was adding two more plates for a total of nine. She turned with a smile to meet her guests. "Hello, there!" she said brightly. "What a pleasant surprise!"

"For us, too," Duffy agreed. Somehow he managed to keep his own smile intact.

Which was more than Mindy Queen was able to manage.

Heaston made the unnecessary introductions. "Mindy's only been here a couple of days herself. When we decided we couldn't stand Guido's pasta any longer, she agreed to become our den mother."

"How lucky can you get! You mean she can cook, too—in addition to looking beautiful?"

Mindy, staring at him with stricken eyes, did not appear to have heard the compliment. Bronko heard, however. "Yeah, she's some dame, all right." His tone turned the remark into a warning that the woman was his property.

There was no doubt that Mindy recognized him. Duffy realized that in another moment she would blurt out the damning revelation; the words were trembling on her crimson lips. When vulnerable, attack . . . and Bronko's jealousy offered him an opening.

He grasped her limp hand and gave it a meaningful squeeze. "Please forgive such a corny line, but haven't we met someplace before? Las Vegas, maybe?"

Mindy was either confused by his boldness or made wary by the warning. Probably the latter, Duffy decided, noting how her glance flicked quickly to Bronko. "Could be," she murmured. "I used to work there. Excuse me, I've got some food on the stove . . ."

So he was off the hook—but for how long? As they washed, he informed Zigonis of their predicament. "I don't think Mindy's part of whatever's going on here. Otherwise, she'd have blown the whistle on us immediately. I've got to convince her that it's in her best interest to keep her mouth shut."

"That's okay for Plan A. How about Plan B? The one that saves our skins if Plan A flops."

"Oh, I don't think we're in any physical danger, whichever way the cat jumps. But damned if I want to lose my cover."

"Better your cover than my neck. I wish I were back in the trailer—and I never thought I'd say that."

Hack and Guido joined the group for lunch. Midway through the meal another Hellion appeared to take the ninth seat at the table. This was Leon Yocum, a skinny taciturn man with a bald head and freckled skin, whom Heaston introduced jovially as "our intrepid birdman." Yocum was the pilot of the helicopter. Duffy knew from his dossier that his commercial license had been revoked following a crash to which alcohol had contributed. However, Yocum was apparently still flying. And obviously still drinking; his lunch consisted of straight whiskey and little else.

Duffy noted one absentee among those he had expected to find at Tres Muertos, the man named Willie Votaw. But since the missing Hellion was not mentioned, he could scarcely raise the question.

The food was served on paper plates family style—appropriately, since indeed the group did give the appearance of a family. If Mindy Queen, at the foot of the table, made a rather unlikely mother, Anthony Heaston, at its head, was the unquestioned father. The others treated him with respect and in the case of Moby Dick, who had been his orderly, with something akin to reverence. They treated one another with the rough camaraderie of brothers, of which Bronko Shaman was the eldest. These men were as different in personality as in appearance, yet they shared a kinship, forged in war and tempered by disgrace, that ran deeper than blood. Duffy, who had never known such a relationship, familial or otherwise, felt a twinge of envy. He even found himself joining in the teasing of the huge albino, the natural butt of their jokes—and, against his will, warming to the compelling personality of the paterfamilias. He was forced to remind himself that if Anthony Heaston was not necessarily his enemy, still he was not his friend.

Friend or enemy, Heaston's charm was undeniable. Articulate and quick-witted, he dominated the table talk, most of which he directed toward his guests. Since Zigonis, playing the role of subservient assistant, kept largely silent, it fell to Duffy to maintain their end.

"The old saloon's held up pretty well, considering," he remarked when the subjects of food and weather had been exhausted. "I thought it might have fallen down by now."

"Then you've been to Tres Muertos before?"

"Only vicariously. My boss, Sheldon Spydell, wrote the last picture to film here—*The Thunder and the Sun*. Maybe you saw it, Colonel."

"Afraid not. I've been out of the country the past few years, mostly in places where they didn't have movie theaters."

"You didn't miss much," Duffy said, glad that the creator was not present to hear the uncharitable opinion. "The picture bombed. Damn near drove us to the wall, in fact."

"In that case, I'm surprised that you'd consider making another one here."

"Well, that's show biz. Always chasing rainbows."

"Must be an interesting life," Heaston observed. "How'd you happen to get into it?"

"I looked around and decided it was the easiest way to make a million bucks without using a gun."

The quip produced a stir it didn't seem to merit. Guido said, "Hey, let us in on the secret formula. What do you need to cut it in Hollywood?"

"The usual. Talent plus brains. Of course, it doesn't hurt a bit if you've got a relative who owns the company." Duffy winked. "Sheldon Spydell is my cousin on my mother's side."

Heaston chuckled. "Back to the salt mines, men. We don't qualify on any of those counts. With the possible exception of the lady. What do you think, Mr. Duffy? Could our Mindy survive in your jungle?"

"I'm sure of it—if she plays her cards right."

"Talk about a stacked deck!" Guido said with a leer. Which drew a laugh from all except Bronko.

And Mindy; she had remained conspicuously mute throughout the meal, scarcely raising her eyes from her plate. Duffy felt sure that she was debating whether to expose him; hence, this second veiled warning. Her furtive glance told him that it had registered, while her murmured "Oh, I'm not so sure I'd be interested" indicated that the issue still hung in the balance. When she began to clear away the dishes, he moved to resolve it in his favor. He followed Mindy into the kitchen on the pretense of refilling his coffee cup.

"Small world, isn't it?"

"Who are you?" Mindy asked in a tense whisper. "What are you doing here?"

"That needn't concern you. Just keep your mouth shut and you won't get hurt."

"Why should I?"

"Because if you spill the beans about me, I'm going to have to tell Bronko that we were shacked up last week in Las Vegas."

"That's a lie!"

"Certainly. But will Bronko think so when I can describe your apartment in detail—down to the brand of Scotch in the bar and the lavender sheets on the bed?"

Mindy gulped. "You wouldn't do a rotten thing like that."

"I'd prefer to be your friend. I've got a hunch you may need one." He removed a Spydell Productions card from his wallet and thrust it into her hand. "If my hunch is right, you can reach me at that address."

She appeared ready to reject both his card and his friendship. "I don't know what you're selling, mister, but I'm not buying it. I'm not afraid of Bronko, either, the way you seem to think, so—"

"I hear my name mentioned?" Bronko had stepped quietly into the kitchen to join them. His suspicious gaze proved that the intrusion was not accidental. "What are you two whispering about?"

The way Mindy shrank back made it equally plain that her bravado was hollow. Since an explanation, true or false, seemed beyond her, Duffy supplied it. "Might as well confess. I was trying to steal your cook. In my opinion, Miss Queen has too much on the ball to waste over a hot stove. I thought she might be interested in a movie career."

"Did you now! And what does she think?"

"I don't believe she's made up her mind yet."

"Yes, I have!" Mindy said quickly. "I'm happy right here. You know that. I wouldn't run out on you, Bronko, not for anything in the world."

"Of course, if you really want to leave—"

"I don't! Believe me, lover, I don't!"

Bronko turned his opaque eyes toward Duffy. "You heard the lady."

"I still think you could do worse, Miss Queen. If you ever change your mind . . ."

Had he won or lost? The answer hinged on how greatly Mindy feared her squat lover's jealousy. As he left the kitchen, Duffy heard Bronko repeat with heavy irony, "If you ever change your mind . . ." The words were followed by the unmistakable sound of an open palm slapping a face. Thanks, Bronko, he thought happily; I needed that. Considering the setting, the hackneyed Hollywood line seemed particularly appropriate.

"When you've finished your coffee," Heaston said, "I'll show you around our little town; that is, if you're interested."

"I am interested," Duffy responded, pushing back his chair. "And I am finished."

"Mind if I stay here?" Zigonis asked. "I've already got a headache and more sun could only make it worse."

The midday sun wasn't actually that hot—but then Zigonis didn't actually have a headache, either. Duffy and Heaston strolled down the wide street, pausing to scrutinize and comment upon the façades and partially complete structures. Duffy was able to identify them all from the movie: the general store and the jail, the opera house and the hotel, the dentist's office, the livery stable and the railroad station. Tres Muertos had changed not one whit in the past six years except to grow older and more shabby. "Sort of an instant ghost town," he observed.

"I bet you're wondering what in the world us ghosts are doing here."

"The question has occurred to me."

"My associates and I intend to restore Tres Muertos to

its former glory. We're going to build a resort here, Mr. Duffy, a combination dude ranch and amusement park for the tourist trade. You can laugh if you like."

"I recall they laughed at Disneyland, too. It does strike me as a big job. Expensive, too."

"You're right on both counts. However, we're not afraid of hard work. And, luckily, we've been able to swing some financial support. We couldn't even begin to attempt a project like this on our own, naturally."

"Seems to me you'd be interested in my proposition, then. We'd pay you a decent price for letting us use the facilities."

"I'm afraid we'd just get in each other's way. Time is of the essence. And, to be truthful, we don't really need the money. Our backing is more than adequate. You'd understand if I could tell you who's involved—but I'm not at liberty to mention names." He added, "I'll appreciate it if you keep what I've told you under your hat. Our agreement stipulates absolutely no publicity until we're much farther along."

"On one condition—that you send me an invitation to the grand opening. When do you expect that to be, by the way?"

"It depends on how things go. We haven't set any exact date. It will be in all the papers when the time comes."

"In that case, I'd better let you get back to work." He had seen everything he had come to see and learned all he could expect to learn. How much or how little that amounted to was yet to be determined.

Heaston did not suggest that Duffy prolong his visit. He bid his guests a cordial farewell on the steps to the saloon and, with Bronko Shaman glowering at his side, watched them out of sight. The jeep escorted them as far as the fence, not merely to see them off the ranch but to make sure that the gate was secured against another such intrusion.

Duffy indicated the briefcase in his companion's lap. "Well?"

"Well, what? I planted the bug. Isn't that what I was supposed to do?"

"Where?"

"Under the dinner table. I figured that was the best spot to pick up conversation. I really would have preferred putting it under the blonde's bed. Now that would be something worth listening to."

"Good show, Neddie. But how did you manage to plant it without anybody seeing you?"

"It wasn't easy, what with five men giving me the fisheye. If it hadn't been for the fire—"

"What fire?"

"The one that broke out in the kitchen a couple of minutes after I went for a drink of water. Ever notice, Jake? Only two things that are guaranteed to distract a man's attention: a girl taking off her clothes and a fire. I couldn't ask Mindy to strip so I dropped an incendiary device with a delayed fuse in the wastebasket. Then I sat back and waited for the stampede." Zigonis shrugged. "But if you ask my opinion—which you haven't—the whole thing was a waste of time and talent."

"You mean you don't expect the bug to work?"

"Oh, it'll work, all right. What I don't expect is that it's going to tell us anything. I've rubbed elbows with a few mobsters in my day. Those men don't fit the mold. Rough and tough, sure, but all in all they come off as a pretty straightforward bunch."

Duffy raised his eyebrows but didn't reply. Zigonis pressed the argument. "Admit it, Jake. You're barking up the wrong tree this time."

"Sorry, Neddie. I'm more convinced than ever that I've got the right tree. Sure, they're a likeable crew, Heaston especially. So were Robin Hood and his merry men—if you happened to be on their side. But I wonder what the Sheriff of Nottingham thought about it?"

Bronko clambered down from the panel truck which housed the shortwave transmitter. "Jeep reports they cleared the ranch and the chopper confirms that they've turned onto the state highway, heading west. Doesn't prove a thing, in my opinion."

Heaston, seated on the rear steps of the saloon, relit his pipe and broke the match before throwing it away. "You still believe they're snoopers?"

"I got to know the Hollywood crowd mighty well working up in Las Vegas. I can spot 'em a mile off, smell 'em farther. Those two ain't it. Not enough of the big I am, know what I mean? They did a sight more listening than talking and that's a sure tipoff."

"Could be they're newspapermen."

"I say they're cops—the same way I say that fire in the kitchen wasn't any accident. God Almighty, Colonel, I was a demolitions expert and if I can't recognize an incendiary when I see it . . . Zigonis set it when he went for that drink of water. He wanted to get the rest of us out of the room. He was the only one who didn't bolt when Mindy started screaming."

Heaston sucked thoughtfully on his pipe. "First the headache so he could stay behind, then the diversion to get rid of the crowd. How long was Zigonis alone?"

"Maybe two minutes, not more than three. As far as I can tell, he never left his chair."

"Then whatever he did, he was able to do right at the table. Offhand, I can only think of three things that might be. First, steal the silverware, which is ridiculous. Second, place a bomb, which is also ridiculous. Third, and not so ridiculous . . ." He left the thought for the other man to complete.

"A bug," Bronko said slowly. "Yeah, that could make it."

Heaston got to his feet. "Suppose we take a look."

Mindy was washing pots and pans in the kitchen while Moby Dick dried them. Heaston paused to knock the residue from his pipe into the wastebasket. "Good lunch, Mindy. I'm sure our guests were impressed. Mr. Duffy was especially complimentary."

"Thanks," she murmured. She did not look at Bronko.

The radio was still playing although the barroom was empty. Heaston turned up the volume then, motioning his companion to maintain silence, approached the harvest table stealthily. Bronko flung back the cloth. Kneeling, they scrutinized the exposed underside of the table. From below, the electronic monitor, no larger than a cigar box, was plainly visible. Adhesive pads held it nestled in the right angle formed by one of the massive legs where it joined the tabletop.

Bronko reached for the gray box but Heaston caught his arm. He replaced the cloth and led the way toward the swinging doors of the saloon. He did not pause on the porch but began to saunter down the street toward the railroad station. Bronko fell into step beside him.

"Recognize it?" Heaston asked. "I do. Pretty sophisticated device, stores up to twelve hours on tape, then surrenders it at high speed by radio to another recorder on a given signal. They're using something similar in the spy-in-the-sky satellites. Big advantage is that you can retrieve the conversation at a time—early morning, say—when it won't interfere with normal radio or television transmissions."

"So how come you wouldn't let me yank it?" Bronko growled, impatient at what seemed to be an ill-timed lecture. "You think it's booby-trapped?"

"No. I was afraid you might break it." Heaston smiled at his bewildered expression. "We've been put under surveillance by the law. Which law we can only guess. Could be Border Patrol, the FBI, Narcotics agents, maybe even the local cops. One thing's definite—somebody's curious about us and what we're doing here. Now we can deactivate their bug, but that won't deactivate their curiosity. I'd rather satisfy it. If we don't, they'll keep trying."

"You mean you're gonna let them listen in?"

"Now we know the bug is there, we can tell it what we want it to hear."

"Colonel, we sit around that table three times a day!" Bronko's eyes narrowed. "I suppose we could put the radio right on top of it—"

"You're missing the point. I want our conversation to come over loud and clear—and so innocuous that it'll bore them to tears."

"I say we're taking a hell of a risk. Suppose somebody spills the beans accidental-like?"

"They won't, not when they know what we know. They're already used to keeping their mouths shut at the table because of Mindy." Heaston's lips curved in a mischievous smile. "The only one who might spill the beans is you, Bronko. Maybe you talk in your sleep."

Bronko bit his lip, more nettled than amused. "I know you didn't like me bringing her here, Colonel."

Heaston shrugged. "Every man has his weakness."

"Yeah. With Moby Dick, it's food. Hack, he's got a thing for killing, same as Yocum for flying. Guido needs money. Me, I need a woman. With you . . ." He hesitated.

"Say it," Heaston invited. "With me, it's glory. Hell, Bronko, you don't have to justify yourself. None of us do—

not as long as we don't put the rest in peril."

"Mindy's too dumb to understand the setup even if I told her straight out. And she's too smart to cross me even if she did understand it."

Heaston clapped his hands together in sudden exhilaration. "Things were running so smoothly that I was beginning to get bored. This makes the game more interesting." He swung around and stared down the dusty street as if expecting to see their enemies through the shimmering haze. "Okay, Mr. Jacob Duffy—you're faded."

George Upp worked in Washington but, like most who could afford it, did not reside there. His home was amid the rolling hills of Maryland, snow-covered this evening, several miles and many tax brackets removed from the capital. Here Upp and his wife lived quietly but elegantly in a gracious two-story mansion which dated back to the early days of the republic, entertaining occasionally but going out seldom.

Tonight was an exception. Upp greeted his visitors in the study, dressed in black tie and smelling of after-shave lotion. "I'm afraid we've come at a bad time," Raymond apologized. "If you'd prefer we see you in town—"

"If I had, I would have told you so on the telephone. My wife and I are attending the grand opening of the Bruegel exhibition at the National Gallery. An obligatory appearance to help place the official stamp of approval on the collection before it begins the tour."

"I read about it, sir. I understand there's never been anything quite like it before."

"So I hear," Upp agreed, his tone indicating that he was no aficionado of paintings. "Anyway, we have plenty of time for a chat. Alice assured me she'll be through dressing in five minutes. From experience I know that means at least thirty." He regarded his other guest with interest. "So you're the famous Jake Duffy I've been hearing about. Or should I make that infamous?"

"That depends on who you care to believe. Me—or the rest of the world."

Upp poured three snifters of brandy. "I gather that you've finally got a wrapup for me on Tony Heaston. I'll be relieved to have this monkey off my back. General Carson's been phoning nearly every day." He sat down in the wingback chair by the fire, crossed his legs and looked expectantly at Raymond.

Raymond cleared his throat, oddly embarrassed. "I'd rather that Jake did the talking. This is his report, not mine." His words indicated that he did not wish to usurp the credit; his tone hinted that he did not care to assume the responsibility, either.

Duffy, still standing, said, "I don't know how much you've been told, sir, so I'll begin at the beginning." He related rapidly but in detail how he had uncovered Anthony Heaston's trail and how he had followed that trail to the secluded ranch on the Mexican border. "That was a week ago today. I've had Heaston and his men under surveillance ever since, both by the bug we planted and by aerial photos—through cooperation of the Navy's air facility at El Centro. I can state definitely that there's something going on at Tres Muertos that bears further invesigagation."

"Um," Upp murmured, grimacing. "I was hoping that you'd be able to give Heaston a clean bill of health. But if you can't, you can't. What do you think he's up to, Duffy? Running narcotics? Smuggling aliens? Or is that ranch the staging area for another one of his squalid foreign adventures—Haiti, perhaps, or Guatemala?"

"Nothing like that. He's going to rob a train."

Upp choked on his brandy. He glanced incredulously at Raymond, who avoided his gaze, and then back to Duffy. "Are you out of your mind? Rob a train! Why, that sort of thing went out with the James brothers. What kind of train? Where?"

"I don't know that yet," Duffy admitted. "But it's the only answer that makes sense."

"It makes no sense at all," Upp snapped. "Good God, man, Heaston is a soldier, not a bloody bandit! We know that somebody went to a lot of trouble and expense to break him out of prison in Colombia. Do you mean to tell me that anyone would do that simply to have him rob a train—a man with no expertise in the field whatsoever? Raymond, do you go along with this fantastic theory?"

"You're saying exactly what I said," Raymond replied uncomfortably. "But Jake's a pretty stubborn boy. I wouldn't even be bothering you with this if you hadn't been pushing me for some kind of report."

"A report, yes. Not a pipe dream."

Duffy, unruffled, said, "I concede your logic, sir. It still doesn't change my opinion. Heaston was busted out of prison to rob a train. For some reason we don't know yet, he's considered essential by whoever is bankrolling the scheme." He paused. "I don't concede that train robbery is passé, though. The biggest crime of the past twenty years was a train robbery, the hijack of the London Mail."

"Different situation altogether. Those men belonged to the underworld. They weren't a bunch of middle-aged ex-soldiers. It's too ridiculous even to discuss." Upp hesitated. "Or do you have some proof you haven't told me?"

"Yes," said Duffy, which drew a pained sigh from Raymond. "Heaston claims that he's developing the ranch as a resort. He isn't. I looked over Tres Muertos personally. It hasn't been changed one iota since the last movie was filmed there—although Heaston and Company have been in residence since early January."

"What about the fence? That's new, isn't it?"

"The fence was installed by a private contractor and finished before Heaston moved in. The only thing they've done in the past two months is to cut firewood and stack it as high as the depot roof. Why? It's not that cold there. Anyway, they use fuel oil for heating and propane for cooking. But that old train burns wood and that's what the lumber pile is being used for. The aerial photos show the train parked in a different spot nearly every day."

"They could be using it to haul materials to wherever they're working."

"Yes—except they're not working anywhere. Look at the total picture, sir. Here we have six men with plenty of money but no visible income. Six men who claim to be building a resort but don't do anything except run a train around a circular track. Six men who wear guns and don't like visitors. Tres Muertos isn't a ranch, it's a training camp, complete with radio-controlled vehicles and an assault helicopter. The thing speaks for itself. Heaston is rehearsing his little army in How to Rob a Train. Oh, one more item. Willie Votaw, the missing member of the old bunch, is a former railroad man. I suspect he's away casing the job."

"Is that what you call proof? I supposed you might at least have learned something from the bug you planted."

"We've drawn a blank there, I admit. Oh, we've gotten plenty of innocent conversation. Maybe a shade too innocent. They haven't talked a bit about what they're doing, the day-to-day activities. I figure they're either being close-mouthed because of Mindy or because they've found the bug, or both."

"Young man," Upp said with an obvious attempt at

patience, "I've been in intelligence work for longer than you've been alive, long enough certainly to recognize the difference between fact and conjecture. You begin with a hypothesis you can't substantiate and proceed to extrapolate from there into the realm of utter fantasy. I admire your ingenuity—but I don't believe a single solitary cotton-picking word of it."

"Nevertheless, I'm right. And I intend to prove it."

"F.X. called you stubborn. I think 'arrogant' is more accurate." Upp carefully set down his brandy glass. "In either case, your connection with this matter is terminated. I intend to report to General Carson that Tony Heaston has been located and that there's no reason to be alarmed."

"Is that what you really believe?" Duffy asked curiously. "Or is it just easier that way?"

Upp sprang to his feet, color flooding his sallow face. Raymond jumped up also. "Jake didn't mean that the way it sounded, sir," he said hastily. "He's been working so damn hard on this thing, been so close to it—"

There was a soft knock on the study door and Mrs. Upp peeked in. "I don't like to interrupt, George, but we really should have left five minutes ago."

"I'll be right with you, dear." Upp managed to get a grip on his anger. "Duffy, I'm going to forget what you said just now. But I warn you not to forget what I said."

Raymond bid him good evening for both of them while steering Duffy firmly toward the door. His smile faded the moment the frigid air struck it, but he did not give vent to his feelings until they were safely down the icy driveway. "You jackass! When are you ever going to learn? You knew that this Heaston case is political dynamite. You were supposed to defuse it, not put a match to it."

"I didn't realize that was General Carson's directive."

"Try to get this through your hard head. George Upp

can do you some good. O.K. Carson can't. He's a dying man—and unless you want to die too, careerwise, you damn well better do what you're told. No more and no less."

"Level with me, F.X. If it was solely up to you, politics aside, would you close the book on Heaston?"

Raymond took a long time to reply. "I don't know. You don't have a shred of proof, Upp's right about that. On the other hand, there's just the barest possibility . . ." He shook his head impatiently. "The question's academic. In the first place, there's no way to put politics aside, especially in government service. In the second place, it doesn't matter what I think—or what you think, either, difficult as that may be for you to accept. The case is closed, Jake."

"Oh, I get the message. But what if Heaston doesn't?"

"Why are you so uptight about it, anyway? You didn't want this assignment in the first place, as I recall."

"Blame my mother. She always made me clean my plate before leaving the table."

"Your mother isn't giving you orders now. I am." He studied the younger man's disgruntled profile. "You've got some leave coming, laddie. Take it. Get out of this miserable climate, find a sunny beach somewhere, Florida or California . . . No, check that. Not California. That's too close to Anthony Heaston. I want you to forget you ever heard his name."

"Whose name?" Duffy managed a wry smile. "You've got to admit I'm trying, at least."

The train rumbled through the night, probing the darkness ahead with a long finger of light, filling the darkness behind with the pungent odor of smoke. The emptiness on either side absorbed the clickety-clack-clickety-clickety-clack of the steel wheels passing over the joints of the track, giving back a pallid echo. The cars rocked to the same monotonous rhythm.

In the distance a second light appeared, the red glow of a fusee placed alongside the tracks. The train commenced to slow in response to the warning, sparks cascading from beneath the huge wheels as the brakes exerted their friction. The engine came to a shuddering stop abreast of the burning fusee while the string of cars it drew took up the slack between them with a series of small jarring crashes.

Before the train had fully conquered the force of momentum, it was itself conquered by another force. From the ditch beside the track where they had lain concealed, five men sprang up. Black jump suits covered their bodies; beneath equally black stocking caps, gas masks concealed their features. Their leader carried a pistol, the remainder were apparently unarmed. Ignoring the engine that was the train's head, they rushed on the cars which formed its body. The leader swung aboard the first Pullman, flung open the door and plunged inside. The others converged on the baggage car immediately behind the engine.

One of the attacking team scrambled up the steel ladder at the rear of the bagagge car. He ran along the roof to the ventilator and pitched a tear gas grenade into the open shaft. The explosion inside was lost in a greater explosion outside. Smoke erupted from a second bomb placed against the baggage car's sliding door.

For a moment, there was silence. Then an arm signal from the man on the roof sent the others, who had retreated to avoid the blast, swarming back to the attack. They flung the sliding door aside and vaulted into the baggage car. From it, they slid an oblong packing case. Their confederate above joined them on the ground to ease the bulky container out the doorway.

The train's whistle blasted twice. It was a signal; the

leader of the gang emerged from the Pullman car. Simultaneously, a sixth jump-suited man leaped down from the cab of the engine. With the others, they began to carry the packing crate at a rapid trot toward the helicopter which waited fifty yards from the track, its rotor blades turning lazily. There was no stumbling or jostling for position; like well-rehearsed pallbearers, each knew his proper position.

They swung the crate aboard the helicopter and followed it through the hatch with the same smooth precision. The rotor blades began to spin faster. The ungainly craft lifted from the earth, executed a graceful pirouette and passed over the looted train like a sated eagle departing from a carcass.

Its passengers tore off their rubber masks, grinning at each other in the gloom, but continued the silence they had maintained throughout the swift and disciplined operation. Bronko finally broke it. "Lay it on us," he invited. "How'd we do?"

Sitting on top the packing case, Heaston lit a match in order to read his stop watch, then used it to fire his pipe. "Six minutes, ten seconds from kickoff to liftoff."

"That's our best time by a full minute. Not bad."

"But still not good enough. We should be able to get it down to five minutes flat with a little more practice."

There was a chorus of groans. Bronko said, "Remember we're one man short. There'll be seven of us when we go up against the real thing."

"Willie won't be able to help us. He'll be doing his own job. It's up to us to do ours. The faster we can do it, the less chance of something going wrong. That's why I'm working your tails off on these dry runs."

"Nobody's really bitching," Moby Dick put in loyally.

"Speak for yourself," Guido retorted. "You got plenty of tail to spare. The rest of us aren't so well-supplied."

He was kidding but Hack was not. "I'm getting sick of waiting for the show to start."

Nodding heads proved he spoke for the others also. "I'm impatient, too," Heaston told them. "But there's nothing we can do about it. We've got to hang loose till we get the word."

They knew that as well as he. However, Moby Dick could not resist asking the question. "How soon do you reckon that'll be, sir?"

"I wish I knew." Heaston stared moodily out the open hatch at the train which sat, empty and motionless, on the desert below the circling helicopter. "All I can say is that it won't be much longer."

TWO

> Well, Hub jumped up in the cab one morn,
> Looked at the sky, said "Sure as I'm born,
> I'll beat God's sun 'cross the western plain,
>   Me and my iron The Gravy Train."
>
> Hub told his fireman: "Pour on the coal!
> Give me steam 'cause I'm fixin' to roll!"
> He sang out loud as they hit the lane,
>   "Sun'll never catch The Gravy Train!"
>
> They jumped one river and then another,
> Gauge read eighty but Hub said, "Brother,
> Shovel faster or I'll sure raise cain,
>   And throw you right off The Gravy Train!"
>
>   —The Ballad of The Gravy Train

"Watch this," Duffy invited. From a kneeling position, he pushed his body upward to the perpendicular and walked on his hands across the sand toward the blanket.

The brown-haired young woman lying there applauded lazily. "Amazing," she murmured. Her name was Barbara Inch. A wide-brimmed straw hat shaded her piquant features from the Florida sun more effectively than the two-piece bikini protected her well-rounded figure—particularly since Barbara had untied the halter in an effort to improve her already superb tan.

He performed a somersault and came to rest in front of her, their faces only a foot apart. "Aren't you going to tell me how wonderful I am?"

Barbara yawned. "It baffles me why you men seem to believe that flexing your muscles arouses a girl."

"Probably for the same reason that you girls seem to believe that taking off your bras arouses a man."

"You mean it doesn't? Hecky darn!" She added, "Anyway, it's not really off, it's just untied."

"Reminds me of when I was a kid. There'd be these girls lying around on the beach with their straps untied, the way yours are. I'd find one who was half-asleep and then I'd pop a paper bag right in front of her. Two out of three times she'd be so startled she'd jump up without remembering to make the necessary adjustments."

"You must have been a rotten kid." But she was unable to contain a giggle. "When did you stop that kind of thing? Or have you?"

"Oh, I quit the moment I discovered there were other ways of achieving the same result. Saved me a fortune in paper bags."

"Hey, look at the time!" She remembered to retie the halter before rising to her knees. "You haven't forgotten that we're joining my folks for cocktails, have you? They're itching to meet the handsome rascal who picked me up at the beach. You did pick me up, you know. Very smoothly, I admit, but it was a deliberate pickup and don't you dare deny it."

"And I thought I was being so subtle. Shucks."

"The only thing I haven't been able to figure out is why? Five days now and you haven't made even one little pass."

"I was hoping I wouldn't have to tell you this, but—well, I'm not like other men. Ever since my accident—"

Her eyes widened. "What accident?"

"Lost my memory. I still pick up girls out of habit—but I can't remember what for."

She threw her beach bag at him. "You rat! You haven't told me one truthful word since we met. Not even where you come from or what you do for a living. All I actually know is that your name is Duffy and you don't live in Fort Lauderdale—and I wouldn't bet on that, either. For all you talk about yourself, you could be a spy."

"Hey, that's pretty close. I'm actually an undercover agent for the Federal Bureau of Investigation."

"Sure you are," she scoffed. "Come on. I'm dying to let Mom and Dad take a crack at you. They're experts at giving my boy friends the third degree. Seriously, though, you'll like my folks. Everyone adores them, even me. But I do want to warn you—please, please, don't get Dad started on the subject of trains. Mom and I have had it morning, noon and night for years and now that his book has made him America's leading authority—"

"Wait a minute. Is your father that Douglas Inch, the one who wrote *Steel Rails and Iron Men?*"

"Yes, Dad's that Douglas Inch."

"No fooling! Funny, I never made the connection until this minute. I remember now that the jacket said he lives here in Fort Lauderdale."

"You mean you've actually read his book?"

"As a matter of fact, I finished it just before I bought my plane ticket. How about that for a coincidence!"

"Train robbery!" Douglas Inch exclaimed, setting down his martini. "You're speaking of a dead art, Jake. Once it was the crime of crimes, at least here in America. We practically invented it, you know. Now it's as extinct as the passenger pigeon."

"Why is that, sir?" Duffy inquired, ignoring Barbara's

pained glance. They sat with their cocktails on the lanai of the comfortable beachfront home a scant hundred yards from the crashing surf. Glass walls muted its thunder and air conditioning repelled its salty fragrance. "The trains are still running, aren't they?"

"Barely. Fifty years ago the train was our principal means of mass transportation. Even as late as World War II there were twenty thousand passenger trains hauling nearly six hundred million people annually—passengers, not commuters. They made an extremely lucrative target. If you couldn't heist a payroll from the baggage car, you could always rob the coaches. Today"—Inch shrugged—"today there are virtually no passengers except on the short-haul commuter trains, and they carry credit cards instead of cash. Payrolls are delivered in armored cars. Even the mail goes mostly by air these days."

Mrs. Inch, a gray-haired copy of her daughter plus twenty-five years and an equal number of pounds, took advantage of the pause to change the subject. "Are you staying long in Fort Lauderdale, Mr. Duffy?"

"I'm not sure. I'm on vacation, but I may have to cut it short."

"Another factor," Inch said, warming to the subject, "is the difficulty. Your nineteenth-century coal burners chugged along at pretty low speeds. They made frequent stops to take on fuel and water. Today's diesel-electrics cruise between ninety and one hundred ten miles per hour—and make practically no stops whatever between division points. Jesse James was able to ride his horse alongside the old Rock Island and board her. Try doing that with the Santa Fe Super Chief!"

"But suppose you substituted a helicopter for the horse? You know, drop a man or two on the roof of the baggage car."

"Possible, I suppose—if your men happened to be circus acrobats. But even if you did manage to drop them onto a narrow platform traveling at a hundred miles an hour, there's still no way for them to get inside."

"Would they have to? Couldn't they detach the baggage car from the train, let it roll to a stop and blast it open at their leisure?"

"I suspect you've seen that in the movies," Inch said in the disparaging tone of the authority. "I doubt if it was ever actually accomplished even in the old days. Our modern coupling devices make it quite impossible now."

"Let's hear it for our modern coupling devices," Barbara muttered.

"You've blighted all my illusions," Duffy complained. "I intended to make train robbery my life work, and here you tell me it's impossible."

Inch chuckled. "That isn't exactly what I said. I said it was difficult. It is, extremely so, but not necessarily impossible. Now if I were going to rob a train, I'd arrange to stop it first, perhaps by manipulating the signals. Of course, I'd pick my spot very, very carefully—some remote area with a long uphill grade and plenty of curves where my train wouldn't be running at its normal speed."

"I'm back in business. You don't happen to know such a spot, do you?"

"Not offhand. And not around these parts, certainly. If there is one, it'd probably be out west someplace."

"What's that noise?" Barbara asked suddenly, causing them all to look at her. "Oh, I know! It's my stomach growling. You did promise to take me out to dinner, didn't you, Jake?"

"Say, I've got a great idea!" her father exclaimed. "Why don't you kids stick around and have dinner with us?"

Mother and daughter exchanged significant glances.

Mrs. Inch said firmly, "I'm afraid I don't have a thing in the house I'd dare offer Mr. Duffy. You two run along."

"Too bad," Inch said with disappointment. "Some other time, then. It's been a pleasure talking with you, Jake. Not often I meet anyone your age who shares my interest in the railroads."

"You've been a big help, sir. I know now how to rob a train and where to do it. All that's left to decide is which train to rob."

"Come on!" Barbara urged, tugging at his arm.

"Oh, your choice is relatively easy," Inch continued as he accompanied them to the door. "You can throw out ninety-nine per cent because their cargo consists of bulk materials—oil and chemicals, ore, automobiles, that sort of thing—that simply aren't practical to steal. How would you ever manage to carry them off?"

"We may be late, Daddy. Don't wait up for me."

"The only exceptions I can think of at the moment are the shipments from the U.S. Mints, Philadelphia and Denver. They still use the trains."

"The U.S. Mint it is. And Denver's out west, isn't it?"

"It was the last time I looked at the map." Inch squeezed his shoulder in mock warning. "But take my advice and forget it. The Mint shipments are under extremely heavy guard, as you can imagine. Why, you'd have to have a small army to take on that kind of job."

"No problem at all. As a matter of fact, Mr. Inch, I know exactly where I can find that small army."

A quarter-mile east of Tres Muertos was a knoll, devoid of vegetation, a reddish-brown prominence which resembled a mole. Some director had chosen it as the site of the Boot Hill without which no western could be complete. A dilapidated picket fence surrounded it. Equally shabby wooden grave markers marched up the slope in sagging ranks like a defeated regiment.

Bronko found his colonel there, moodily studying the inscriptions. "Ever read any of these?" Heaston asked. "Some are classics. 'Mexican Joe, Horse Thief. Hung High, Buried Deep.' Or that one over there. 'Here lies the cardsharp Hendry Jones—his deck was cold and so's his bones.' "

"Nobody's really buried here, are they?"

"Probably not. Wouldn't be surprised if the inscriptions are authentic, though. They have that ring. Those old pioneers had a strong sense of humor."

Bronko grunted. "I never saw much to laugh at in a cemetery."

"Why not? Might as well laugh while you can."

However, Heaston's tone was morose. Bronko recognized that he was sunk in one of his periodic fits of melancholy. "Something gnawing on you?"

"Barracks fever, I guess. I couldn't manage the siesta today so I decided to take a walk." He continued his stroll, pausing to regard each grave marker intently, almost as if he expected to find his own name on one. But when he spoke again, it was with his customary crispness. "Well, Bronko, what did you learn?"

"The trailer's cleared out. I covered the area outside the fence all the way to the main road. You handled it right, Colonel. Fed 'em enough drivel until they got tired listening to it. Now we can get rid of that damn bug."

"No, I intend to keep it. That bug is somebody's property. You wouldn't want Duffy to think we're common thieves, would you? We'll return it to him at the appropriate time—with an appropriate message."

"Like what?"

"How about 'I've Been Working on the Railroad'? In

seven-part harmony."

Bronko chuckled. "God, I'd like to be there to see his face! At least, we can deactivate it, can't we? Tell the truth, I've been watching my words so careful that I haven't been able to enjoy my food."

"We're still going to have to watch our words," Heaston said, giving him an odd glance. "We can deactivate the bug—but who's going to deactivate Mindy?"

"I told you not to worry about her. She's too dumb to read the score."

"I know—and too scared of you to do anything about it, anyway. I'm afraid you may have underestimated her, Bronko. While Mindy was in Calexico this morning buying groceries, Dick saw her mail a letter. That's bad enough, but the way she did it—when she thought he wasn't looking—makes it worse. Of course, maybe she just wanted to tell Mother that her little girl is having a wonderful time here on the ranch."

"Mindy don't have a mother. No family at all. Just an ex-husband and she hates his guts."

"Maybe a friend, then?"

"Maybe," Bronko muttered. He kicked the nearest grave marker savagely, sending it bouncing down the hillside. "And I guess I'd damn well better find out who that friend might be."

The United States Mint in Denver plays host to over 200,000 sightseers per year, making it the mile-high city's prime tourist attraction. The visitors come to the massive granite blockhouse to view the production line which turns out three billion coins annually and to stare reverently at the display of gold ingots, a tiny fraction of the bullion—nearly one-quarter of the nation's monetary gold reserves—which lies in the vaults below. Few receive a personally conducted tour from the superintendent, however.

Palmer Eubanks led Duffy down a long corridor to a large room where punch presses filled the air with a staccato hammering. "Pennies," he explained above the din, gesturing at the copper which entered the presses as a great sheet and emerged as a torrent of shiny blank disks. "Up to eighteen million of them every day." Beyond the presses were other machines, nearly as noisy, which annealed and cleaned and stamped heads and tails on the blanks, while a final device sorted out the defective coins.

"What? No samples?" Duffy asked as they reached the comparative hush of the superintendent's office.

Eubanks grinned. "Not even for the FBI. I hope you weren't expecting any."

"I wasn't. I wasn't expecting snow, either." In his rush to catch the plane, Duffy had neglected to don winter garb. The lightweight sport coat which had been too warm for Florida was scant protection against the icy winds of Colorado. "I'd better get my business done before I start sneezing."

"Good idea. Time is money, and nowhere is that more true than here."

"It's money I want to talk to you about. Specifically, I'd like some information on how and when you people ship it. Also where."

Eubanks raised his eyebrows. "How specific should I be? I can give you a detailed breakdown of our operation covering the past twenty-five years or any portion of it, if you're willing to wait a bit."

"Just a general outline will be plenty."

"You asked for the how, when and where of it. Let's start with how. Our shipments leave Denver almost exclusively by train except on rare occasions when there's a rush order. Then we use air freight."

"Would that be a special train?"

"Oh, no. We have our own spur line and our own baggage cars. They're loaded and sealed here. When we're ready to ship, a switch engine picks up the car and hooks on to a regularly scheduled train." Eubanks hesitated. "If the FBI is concerned about the security practices here at the Mint—"

"The FBI isn't. Anyway, as we're both aware, that's the Treasury Department's bailiwick."

"Now as to where we ship. The Denver Mint supplies the principal Federal Reserve banks west of the Mississippi, approximately twenty in all. They in turn distribute to the other banks in their region. The greatest demand, of course, comes from those regions with the greatest population, California, for example—although Nevada, merely because of Reno and Las Vegas, requires more than its per capita share."

"Las Vegas," Duffy said thoughtfully. "How often do you ship there?"

"We don't. Las Vegas is supplied by the Federal Reserve depository in Los Angeles, just as Reno is serviced from San Francisco. Have I said something to disappoint you, Mr. Duffy?"

"I'll get over it. Please go on."

"Well, I've covered how we ship and where we ship. As to when . . . we have no fixed schedule. Both what the Mint coins—the denominations and the amounts—and when we coin it depends entirely upon the demand. That fluctuates greatly. We do maintain a certain minimum level of output, naturally, based on what we know from experience to be the average life of our product. But we try to keep our inventory small. Any overage is stockpiled here until it's needed." Eubanks spread his hands. "I think that covers it. Now would you mind telling me why you wanted to know?"

"We've gotten certain information which leads us to believe that a big heist is in the works, probably involving a train, possibly somewhere in the western United States. I'm working on the angle that a shipment from the Denver Mint is the target."

"What makes you think so?"

"Process of elimination. The Denver Mint's in the western United States. You ship by train. And your shipments are among the few cargoes today both valuable enough and practical enough to heist."

"I'd be inclined to debate that last point. Our shipments are valuable enough—though perhaps not as valuable as you assume. The average runs to around a million dollars. Anything over that would be exceptional."

"Guess it all depends on the point of view. Most people wouldn't consider a million bucks anything to sneeze at."

"I think it depends more on what form the million comes in. Coins have little real value in themselves, except to collectors, particularly these days when we've replaced all the gold and most of the silver with alloys. What can you do with one hundred million pennies—except put them into parking meters? Nickels and dimes aren't much more useful. Even quarters have to be converted into dollars before you can spend them conveniently. And that—plus a small number of half-dollars—is all the Denver Mint coins and ships. We haven't minted dollars in years. Currency, of course, is handled by the Bureau of Engraving. What I'm saying, Mr. Duffy, is that if you should hijack one of our shipments, you'd have a devil of a time doing anything with it. You'd have to change it into paper money before it was really useful. That would take years."

"How about the foreign markets?"

"The basic problem is the same anywhere. Assuming

that you could smuggle the coins abroad, you'd still have to convert them. No foreign bank would touch them. I doubt if the black market would be much more receptive, either."

"I've got to admit that your rebuttal makes sense, Mr. Eubanks. I came hootin' out here, sure that I had the answer, but now . . ." Duffy sighed. "And to think that I gave up a warm beach and a pretty girl for nothing except the chance to catch pneumonia!"

Dozing, Mindy sensed rather than saw that the bedroom light had been turned on. Bronko was finally coming to bed. For a moment, she debated keeping her eyes shut in the hope that he, thinking her asleep, might not disturb her. She knew the deception was useless. Might as well get it over with; Mindy put on a drowsy smile. "Hi," she murmured. "Been dreaming about you."

"Sure you have, baby." His ironic tone disturbed her. Squinting, she was surprised to discover that he was still fully dressed. Bronko stood above the bed less like her lover than her executioner.

Mindy opened her mouth to ask what was wrong. Before her lips could form the words, the sheet which covered her was stripped away. One of Bronko's hands closed on her throat, jerking her upright. The other slapped her viciously.

"That was just to get your attention." He spoke in a voice barely above a whisper, but in Mindy's shocked ears it rang as loud as a shout. "Now suppose you tell me about that letter."

"What—what letter?"

His fingers dug deeper into her throat. "You know damn well what letter! The letter you mailed this morning, that's what letter!"

Choking, she tried to escape the strangling grip. Bronko held her captive a moment longer, then hurled her back onto the pillow. "Knock off the sobbing. That's nothing to what you're gonna get for crossing me."

"Don't hurt me!" she whimpered, squirming as far from him as the headboard would permit. "I haven't crossed you —I swear I haven't!"

"Yeah? What about the letter?"

Mindy hesitated, fumbling for an explanation that would placate him. The bedroom confrontation, numbing in its suddenness, had left her as naked of invention as she was of body. She realized that Bronko had intended it so. As he took a menacing step toward her, she cried out, "I can explain about that if you'll only let me!"

"I'm listening."

"Well, it—it wasn't anything bad. Just a letter to a friend of mine in L.A. Somebody I used to work for before I came to Vegas." Since he appeared to accept that, she was emboldened to add, "He owes me money and I thought—"

"What's this friend's name?"

"It wouldn't mean anything to you. You've never met him."

"Sure about that?" And Mindy saw to her horror that he held the business card of Spydell Productions, Inc., which Duffy had given to her.

The men seated around the long table could have been a board of directors listening soberly to their chairman report a decline in net earnings. They were, in fact, a jury.

The foreman concluded his review of the evidence. "So what we face here is a possible breach of our security. Possible—because we can't be certain what was in that letter. If we accept Mindy's story that she wrote Duffy she wanted to take up his offer of a screen test—"

"Bat crap!" Bronko said. "We know Duffy ain't no producer."

"The question is: Does Mindy? Did she write to Duffy because she thought he was a producer—or because she knew he was a cop?"

"Why don't we ask her?" Moby Dick ventured.

The naive suggestion produced smiles around the table. "Now how come I didn't think of that?" Guido wondered. "Dick, you're a genius!"

"I say she's lying all the way," Hack muttered.

"Let's assume for a minute that Hack's right," Heaston said. "What does Mindy know that is going to hurt us? In other words, could she have told Duffy anything beyond what he already suspects? Bronko swears he hasn't spilled the beans. How about the rest of you? Speak up," he urged, studying their troubled expressions. "Dick, you've spent more time with her than anyone else, Bronko excepted. What have you two talked about while you washed the dishes?"

The albino licked his white lips with an equally colorless tongue. "I don't remember. We just talked, you know, about things."

"Such as what you were going to do after you leave here?"

"No, sir! Oh, maybe in a general sort of way. I mean, not about the train—I wouldn't do that—but about, well . . ."

"How you mean to spend your million bucks?" Guido suggested slyly.

"I didn't! I never once told her how much it's gonna be!"

Bronko jumped to his feet. "You tub of lard! I should have known you couldn't keep that fat trap shut!"

"At ease!" Heaston ordered sharply. "I've got a sneaking suspicion that Dick isn't the only one with a loose lip. How about it? Guido?"

"Okay," Guido admitted with a shrug. "We've ridden into town a couple of times together. You've got to talk about something, don't you? Maybe I did drop a few hints here and there."

His admission prompted sheepish confessions from the others. Each man, given the feminine audience, had responded as men usually do, by talking about himself—although each maintained that he had divulged nothing of their mission. "Looks like we're all guilty," Heaston said wryly. "Including you, Bronko, or I miss my guess. Individually, none of us spilled very much. But add it up—and what we haven't told her, she may have figured out. She'd have to be blind and deaf not to know about the train."

"Sunk by a dame," Hack groaned.

Yocum pushed back his chair. "I move we cut out while we still can."

"No way, Ace. We've got to sit tight until we get the go signal. Not to mention Willie's scouting report. Scatter now and we've lost the bloody ball game. Anyhow, I don't see any cause to panic. Duffy was already suspicious of us. The worst Mindy's letter can do is make him more suspicious. But suspicions alone aren't enough. There's no way on earth he can figure out what we mean to do until we actually do it. By then it'll be too late."

Guido looked dubious. "Begging your pardon, Colonel, but maybe the rest of us understand the fuzz better than you. I've been busted more than once on nothing stronger than suspicion."

"That's for sure," Hack agreed. "And with the broad as a witness—"

Bronko slammed his fist onto the table. "Let's quit beating around the bush. We got to shut her up. I was the one who brought her here and I'm the one who'll get rid of her. Hack, you and me'll—"

"Hold it!" Heaston snapped. "I'm still running this outfit, Bronko. I'll give the orders. If I understand your suggestion, you want us to—what was that marvelous phrase the CIA used?—terminate with extreme prejudice."

Bronko flushed at the reprimand. "Put it any way you like."

"I'll put it this way: Your suggestion stinks. Maybe the rest of you have forgotten a man named Do Binh. I haven't. I don't mean to go down that road again. We may be forced to kill someone before this is over—but there'll be no more executions while I'm in command." He glared around, daring dissent; finding none, he went on in a milder tone, "At the same time, we can't permit Mindy to continue on here."

"You saying we should just give Mindy her walking papers?" Bronko asked. "That idea stinks worse than mine."

"Walking papers," Heaston repeated thoughtfully. "Now you're talking, Bronko. I think Mindy's earned a vacation. Baja California would be ideal, some little village with plenty of peace and quiet—but with no roads or telephones or mailboxes. When's the next flight south, Ace?"

Yocum shrugged. "This airline's strictly non-sked. You name it."

"First thing in the morning will be fine. The lady has another letter to write." Heaston began to smile. "We wouldn't want Mr. Duffy to waste his valuable time coming down here to look for her, would we?"

The compromise solution won approval that ranged from enthusiastic to grudging. Moby Dick voiced the only regrets. "I reckon we got to do it," he said with a sigh. "But I sure am gonna miss her cooking."

Duffy sat at the lunch counter in the Denver air terminal, his mood as bleak as the weather outside and his reflections as bitter as the coffee he sipped. The expedition west, begun with high hopes and against orders, had ended as a fiasco. Like the prospectors who had worked these Colorado mountains, he had pounced on what appeared to be a priceless nugget only to have the assay prove it worthless. Unlike those prospectors, he could not go confidently on to the next mountain; he was out of mountains.

Most men would have told themselves that they had done the best they could and, absolved, accepted the disappointment philosophically. Duffy could not. Since he remained convinced of the validity of his theory, lack of a single shred of proof notwithstanding, failure merely demonstrated that he had not done the best he could. Others had accused him of taking his work too personally, and they were right. He viewed each assignment not as a job, as most did, or as a game, as some did, but as a duel. In Anthony Heaston, the man so like himself, Duffy sensed that he had found a worthy opponent. To concede now, to be content with the pallid vindication of I-told-you-so at some future date . . . Yet what choice did he have? His thoughts, fueled by frustration, traveled a well-worn circular track like the train at Tres Muertos and, like it, returned inevitably to the same starting place.

There was nothing for him to do but to slink back to Florida. Barbara Inch was miffed, no doubt, by his precipitous departure ("You might at least have had the decency to tell me!" et cetera, et cetera), but he could probably charm his way into her good graces—and her bed as well. The prospect gave him no pleasure. Sexual satisfaction was measured in minutes at most. Whipping Anthony Heaston and his hard-bitten guerrillas was something a man could savor for a lifetime.

Duffy strolled out into the terminal and discovered that his flight, already delayed by the storm, had been set back yet another thirty minutes. To kill the time, he bought a magazine at the newsstand and weighed himself on the scales which also told his fortune; neither reading excited him. With twenty of the thirty minutes still remaining, he leaned against the bank of lockers out of the way of the human traffic which ebbed and flowed through the huge lobby. He really did feel punk, he decided, and wondered if this was the result of depression or whether the sudden change of climate had caused him to contract a virus. Whichever, it was a lousy world.

He was further disgruntled to learn that the locker against which he leaned was the very one, of the hundred or more available, which the man approaching, key in hand, wished to open. Wearily, he stepped aside.

He would not have given the stranger a second glance had not the man sneezed suddenly. The explosion, both startling and annoying in its proximity, caused Duffy to regard him sharply. As he stared, the man sneezed again.

"Bless you!" Duffy said warmly.

The sneezer, a gaunt middle-aged man with a large nose and a prominent Adam's apple, smiled sheepishly. "Thanks. This damn weather . . . I'll be glad to get out of it."

"Where you heading?"

"L.A.—if I don't miss my plane." He removed a bulging suitcase from the locker and hastened away toward the far end of the terminal.

"Bless you," Duffy murmured again. The benediction was not meant in its conventional sense; it was his way of giving thanks. The sneezer was Willie Votaw, the seventh and heretofore missing member of Heaston's Hellions.

There was no time to speculate on the devious twist of fate which had led Votaw to this particular spot at this particular movement. There was barely enough time to take advantage of it. He strode after the retreating figure, his malaise forgotten, and joined the line in which Votaw stood.

The reservations clerk, more harried than usual by the storm-created problems, was understandably annoyed to be confronted by another. Yes, there was a seat available on the flight to Los Angeles and, yes, a switch of tickets could be arranged, providing Mr. Duffy was willing to pay the differential. However, the clerk refused to guarantee that Mr. Duffy's baggage, which might already be aboard his original flight, could be transferred as readily. He looked disappointed when the dour warning had no effect.

Duffy was the last passenger to board the huge jet. He barely fastened his seat belt before the aircraft lumbered away from the terminal. He had lost sight of Willie Votaw while waiting for his ticket to be exchanged; he was relieved to spy the gaunt man three rows in front of him. The duel wasn't over, after all. Fate had presented him with an unexpected reprieve. While he wasn't sure yet how to exploit it, he had nearly three hours and half a continent in which to find a way.

The airlines had its own plans for his time. Once the jet reached its assigned altitude and cruising range, once the crew introductions had been made and the flight data announced, screens were lowered. Those not interested in the film were free to listen to three channels of recorded music and one of recorded comedy, to read or to doze. Dinner would be served upon conclusion of the movie; in the meanwhile, passengers were invited to visit the lounge.

He was not surprised to see Willie Votaw heed the call to the bar. The former guerrilla had the jittery manner of one who endures rather than enjoys flying. To such persons bottled liquor is more diverting than canned entertainment. Duffy waited five minutes and followed him.

Votaw occupied a padded bench against the forward bulkhead. Although his tenure had been brief, he was already sipping his second cocktail. Duffy ordered one for himself. "Mind if I join you?"

"Help yourself," Votaw replied, making room on the bench. "I should warn you, though, I may be coming down with—" His red-rimmed eyes widened in recognition. "Say, aren't you the fellow, the one back at the terminal?"

"Bless you," Duffy agreed with a smile. "How you feeling by now?"

"God-awful. I wasn't prepared for a blizzard."

"Then Colorado isn't your home, either?" Duffy extended his hand. "My name's Rush. Jerry Rush."

Votaw withdrew his clammy palm in order to blow his nose. "William Votaw."

"What takes you to California? A little vacation?"

"Don't I wish it. Nope, it's a business trip. Got to check into my firm's head office."

"Aerospace? That seems to be the big thing out there."

"Land use and development. The HH Company—I doubt if you ever heard of us. Not many people have."

Duffy admitted that he belonged to the majority and let the conversation languish for a moment lest Votaw suspect that it was, in truth, an interrogation. He drained his cocktail before continuing, "Land use and development. Is that just another way of saying the real estate business?"

"In this case, it's another way of saying the mining business."

"Really? Funny, I'd never have tabbed you for a miner."

"You're so right. Don't catch me digging holes in the ground. I just tell other folks where. Mineral surveys, that's my racket." He shrugged when Duffy commented that it must be an interesting profession. "A lonely one, anyway. I've been on this one better than a month, must have covered five thousand miles all told. I'm looking forward to chucking it, and soon. If things pan out the way I expect, I'll be able to retire."

"Sounds like you must have struck gold." He nudged Votaw slyly. "Wouldn't care to tell me where, would you?"

"Professional secret, Mr. Rush. Yeah, I found what I was looking for, all right. Not gold, though." He added with a wink, "But I guess everything turns to gold eventually if you're lucky."

"Long time yet before I can even think of retiring myself. When that day comes, I've got eyes to do a little traveling. Not this way—this isn't really traveling, just a means to get from one place to the next—but some way that'd let me see where the hell I was."

"Yeah. Flying's for the birds, and that's all it's for."

"For my money, nothing beats the train. Particularly out west. There's an awful lot of beautiful scenery down there. Not to mention that I haven't heard of anybody hijacking a train to Cuba."

For the first time, the normally congenial Votaw appeared wary. "I guess you're right. Haven't ridden a train in years myself."

His obvious uneasiness at the mention of trains told Duffy what he wanted to know; to probe further would be unwise. He turned the conversation to a safer topic. "Ever do any fishing, Mr. Votaw? I was down in Florida just last week, managed to bag myself a marlin . . ."

Votaw, as Duffy knew from his dossier, was an ardent angler. Any latent suspicion melted away in the enthusiasm kindled by his favorite sport. Duffy, who could not tell a bonefish from a red snapper, listened with outward fascination and inward resignation to blow-by-blow accounts of past contests, prizes captured and even larger which had escaped. The announcement that dinner was being served finally rescued him.

"Been a real pleasure," Votaw assured him as they parted. "Maybe we can pick up where we left off after chow."

"Afraid we'll be in L.A. by then. Could be we'll run into each other some other time, though."

Votaw, who believed it highly unlikely, said that he certainly hoped so. Duffy, who considered it completely probable, echoed the sentiment. He ate his steak without really tasting it while his mind chewed on what he had learned. Most of Votaw's story was false, of course, yet there was enough truth mingled in to allow him to draw certain conclusions. The HH Company has dispatched him on a scouting expedition—not only extensive but apparently successful—and Votaw was returning to present his report. Since he carried no briefcase, that report might be contained in his head. On the other hand, it might not.

When the tray was removed, Duffy strolled aft on the pretext of visiting the rest room. Making sure that Votaw was not watching him, he ducked into the galley instead.

The pert stewardess looked startled. "I'm sorry, sir, but passengers are not permitted—"

Duffy held his identification at eye level. "FBI. I need to get a message to the flight deck immediately."

The face beneath the perky cap went pale as her mind jumped to the natural, yet erroneous, conclusion. "Oh, God!" she whispered. "You don't mean we're being—"

"Hijacked? No, nothing like that. I want you to ask the captain to radio ahead to L.A. International and arrange for all off-loaded baggage from this flight to be held for inspection. Without informing the passengers, of course.

Will you do that for me?"

The stewardess nodded, yet she was far from being reassured. "You think—" she began and had to moisten her lips before continuing. "You think there's a bomb aboard?"

"I certainly hope not." He patted her shoulder comfortingly. "Relax, darling. All I'm after is a little piece of paper."

Duffy stood in the ground-level baggage room of the terminal building and watched the mini-tractor drag its train of carts, piled high with suitcases, alongside the conveyer belt which led to the claiming area outside.

The supervisor of baggage operations fidgeted unhappily at his side. "How long is this going to take, anyway?"

"Depends on whether the suitcase I'm looking for is on the top or on the bottom. Have your boys line 'em up on the floor."

Willie Votaw's suitcase was not immediately visible among the hundred or more the carts carried. However, Duffy was pleased to spy his own; it had made its owner's flight, after all.

"Another couple of minutes and Upstairs'll be screaming bloody murder."

"Won't be the first time passengers have had to sweat out their luggage."

"Yeah, but the company makes a big selling point about us being different. No waiting, no delays, that sort of crap. We get marked down if it doesn't reach the pickup dock before—"

"There it is!" Duffy darted forward and plucked Votaw's bulging suitcase from the grasp of the skycap.

"Hallelujah! Okay, men, get the rest of the load onto the belt."

"Check that! It's all got to go together. If everybody else gets his luggage and my man doesn't, he's bound to wonder why."

The SBO struck his forehead with a groan and stamped off a few paces. He came back to stand over Duffy who, kneeling on the concrete floor, was attempting to wrench open the suitcase. "Locked, naturally," Duffy murmured. He searched his pockets for the tiny pick he normally carried.

The telephone jangled, its bell as loud as a burglar alarm. The SBO went to answer it, cursing under his breath. "I know, I know!" he informed his caller. "We're doing the best we can but we got problems." He covered the mouthpiece to relay the question. "How much longer? I've got to tell them something."

The lock gave; Duffy threw back the lid. "Tell them five minutes." The suitcase contained the usual assortment of clothing and gear, a suit and two sweaters on hangers, a pair of shoes wrapped in a towel, toilet articles in a fake leather case, shirts and pajamas and socks and underwear, mostly soiled. The bulging appearance derived less from the amount the suitcase carried than from the careless manner in which it was packed; Votaw was not a tidy traveler.

"Find it yet?" the SBO inquired hopefully, without the faintest notion of what "it" amounted to.

Duffy, who had only a slightly better notion, shook his head and continued to rummage, hampered by the necessity of replacing each article in its original place. It seemed unlikely that Votaw would notice that his already jumbled belongings had been rifled, but he could not risk the possibility.

He was almost ready to give up when his fingers, pawing through the all-too-ordinary contents, encountered something that was not. It was a square of flexible plastic about the size of a large pocket handkerchief, not hidden exactly but tucked—perhaps for protection—in the folds of a freshly pressed shirt.

"What you got?" the SBO asked, craning over his shoulder.

His first thought—more accurately, his hope—was that he had discovered a map. The plastic had been marked in black grease pencil with a series of apparently haphazard X's and O's. There were numbers also, five or six digits divided by a dash and a colon, such as 120—1:37. From them extended arrows which led nowhere. It was not a map, he realized, but the transparent overlay to a map. One was intended to complement the other; individually, each was as useless as a bolt without its nut.

Yet since the bolt was missing, he must make what he could of the nut. "You got a photocopier here?"

The SBO slapped his pockets. "Now that's funny. Must have left it in my other pants. Hell, no, I don't have any damn photocopier!"

Upon questioning, he guessed that the nearest such device was located in the offices upstairs—and those offices were probably closed. With time short, Duffy chose the first alternative which came to mind. He spread his handkerchief (fresh, luckily) on top of the plastic and in ball-point pen traced an overlay of the overlay. He replaced the transparency in its former hiding place, locked the suitcase and told the SBO, "Take it away. Sorry if I've caused you any inconvenience."

"Inconvenience I can live with. But if my wife doesn't get the bonus I've been promising her . . ."

Duffy slipped out by a side exit and joined his fellow passengers at the pickup dock. He saw Willie Votaw among them but did not attempt to approach him. The delayed luggage was just commencing to arrive via the conveyer belt to be greeted with exclamations of relief and indignation. Duffy added his voice to the chorus.

The helicopter returned after nightfall. Bronko met it in the jeep in order to illuminate the landing pad with the headlights. At least, that was the reason he gave the others.

Hack was out the hatch before the rotor blades ceased turning. He bent to pat the earth lovingly. "Never again," he vowed. "I can take an hour or two, but a full day . . . Jesus!"

"How'd it go?"

"Okay." He commenced to do deep knee bends to relieve his cramped muscles. "Must have twisted my back," he complained with a grimace.

Bronko seized his arm angrily. "Okay? What kind of an answer's that?"

"Well, what kind of an answer do you want? I did what you told me to do, what else? You don't see her in the chopper, do you?"

"Any problems?"

"Not with me." Hack jerked a thumb at the helicopter. "Maybe you better talk to Ace, though. He don't act too happy."

Bronko climbed the ladder and went forward to the flight deck. The engine had long since ceased and all switches were off, but Yocum continued to slouch in the pilot's seat. He jumped when Bronko touched his shoulder. "You all right, Ace?" Yocum shook his head miserably, not looking at him. "Brought this along," Bronko said, producing a half-pint of bourbon from his hip pocket. "Figured you might need a drink."

Yocum seized the bottle and drained a respectable portion of its contents. "Thanks," he said with a shudder for which the whiskey was not entirely responsible. "Bronko, did you know about this ahead of time?"

"Now that's a foolish question," Bronko reproved in a mild voice. "You didn't suppose Hack was acting on his own, did you?"

"But we agreed last night—The Colonel said—"

"I know what the Colonel said. Happens I said different. Look at me, Ace! Heaston's a fine soldier, but he's got a lot to learn about this business. When you find a squealer, you don't let her off with a slap on the wrist. You fix her so she can't squeal no more ever."

"There's going to be hell to pay when the Colonel finds out."

"Who's going to tell him? Not me. Not Hack. Not you, either. I wouldn't take kindly to that at all. Anyway, where's the point? What's done is done." He put a hand on the pilot's shoulder and shook him gently. "Snap out of it, buddy. Not as if you haven't done your share of killing here and there. Women, too, if I remember rightly."

"That was different," Yocum muttered.

"Different, my foot! You sound like Heaston. Time people woke up. We're putting our necks on the block here same as back in Nam. And we had to get rid of Mindy for the same reason we gunned down those dinks—to keep our necks from being chopped off. Okay, so you didn't enjoy it then and you don't enjoy it now. Who does?"

"Hack does. He was laughing when he pushed her out."

"Would it have made you feel better if he'd been bawling?"

Yocum's voice shook with mingled anger and revulsion. "But did he have to lay her first? Was that necessary, too?" He commenced to retch.

There was a moment of silence; Bronko's explosive laugh broke it. "So that's how he hurt his back! Well, why not? That's all she was good for, anyway."

Yocum stared at him incredulously. "I thought you liked her a lot."

"More than some and less than others. Got to be realistic, Ace. You can always pick up another broad—but how many chances do you have to pick up a million bucks?" Bronko got to his feet. "The Colonel's waiting to hear all about that picturesque little village where Mindy's spending her vacation. I'd rather you did the talking. Hack might blow it."

"What do you want me to say?"

"Oh, stick with the truth as far as you can. Say that you dropped her off someplace in the mountains."

Duffy lingered at the international airport long enough to see Willie Votaw off again. He was careful to remain at a discreet distance from his quarry, nor did he consider following him farther. Votaw's flight was headed for Yuma, which made his ultimate destination obvious. The Tres Muertos ranch was only an hour's driving time from the Arizona city. Continued surveillance was unnecessary.

His sudden change of plans had caused him to arrive in Los Angeles without a hotel reservation. Recalling his promise to his cousin, he telephoned the Spydell residence. He didn't have to ask for lodgings; Selena issued the invitation like a command.

Most of the city known as Beverly Hills is (oddly enough, although its inhabitants don't appear to find it so) located on the flatlands. The Spydells lived among the hills from which the region took its name. The Tudor-style home, clinging precariously to a slope at the end of a winding lane, could not precisely be called a mansion; however, the description would do until the real thing came along. Sheldon Spydell had not built the two-story structure, planted the ivy or installed the swimming pool.

In fact, the house was commonly referred to as "So-and-So's old place," So-and-So being the former and otherwise forgotten movie star who had shot himself to death in an upper bedroom. There was a rumor that his ghost still haunted the grounds.

The present mistress of the manor took no stock in ghosts; had one appeared at her door, she would have invited him in for a drink. Nothing upset Selena Spydell and certainly not a distant relative, suitcase in hand. She was a chic matron of considerable charm and unflagging energy who wore the fashions of California but retained the inflections of the Bronx.

"Shelly's not home yet," she informed Duffy. "I used to think it was bad when he was just a writer, always around the house. Now I call them the good old days. Since he became a producer, I see the milkman oftener than I do him."

Duffy was surprised to learn that his arrival hadn't been completely unexpected. Selena produced the reason—two letters addressed to him at Spydell Productions. "Shelly figured you must becoming back soon or you wouldn't have told them to write to you here."

Since he could not recall giving anyone those instructions, he studied the envelopes with a puzzled frown. Then he saw the postmarks. Calexico, California. Mindy Queen, of course. He tore open the letter with the earlier date.

>   *Dear Mr. Duffy—*
>   *You said I should write you if I ever needed a friend and I guess maybe I do!! Something's going on here I don't like. I don't know what it is exactly cause nobody'll tell me right out except it must be something awful big and I mean BIG!! I don't want nothing to do with anything that's against the law and I'd like to cut out but Bronko'd skin me alive if he ever knew I was thinking*

about it so I wondered if maybe you could help me somehow and then maybe I could help you, know what I mean? Only when you come back here please don't let on it was me who asked you to, okay? Very truly yours,

Mindy Queen.

P.S. Does the name Mr. Zoose mean anything to you? I heard it said a couple of times when they didn't think I was listening.

The second letter, postmarked a day later, bore little relation to the first. The message was shorter and the tone formal, conveying none of the panic of its predecessor. Even the handwriting, although still Mindy's, was different. The first was written in a hasty scrawl; the second appeared to have been composed at leisure. Mindy asked him to please disregard her earlier letter. Since writing it, the situation had changed. She was leaving the ranch—would, in fact, be gone by the time he received this—so she would be unable to take advantage of his offer.

The two letters appeared to cancel each other out. One begged for his help, the sequel dismissed it. Which was he to believe? It didn't seem to make much difference. He doubted if Mindy could tell him more of Heaston's plans than he had already deduced on his own. He dared not return to Tres Muertos now, in any case. His mission was to foil a train robbery, not to ride to the rescue of fair damsels, who might neither need nor welcome rescue.

Besides, he was bone-weary. During the past twenty-four hours he had crossed the continent with precious little sleep to sustain him. He entreated Selena to bid her husband both hello and good night on his behalf, and trudged up to the guest room. The bed was made up, the covers turned back. Selena, thorough in her hospitality as in everything, had placed an assortment of magazines and a bottle of cognac on the nightstand.

His suitcase was nearly as untidy as the one he had searched earlier, containing mostly dirty clothes. All were drip-dry fabrics, veterans of many a hotel room laundering, but Duffy was too tired to tackle the chore tonight. While undressing, he spread out his handkerchief on the dresser, trying to make something of the cryptic symbols and numbers. Even this demanded more energy than he possessed.

However, as sometimes happens, he was unable to fall asleep. His body cried for rest but his mind would not surrender. He switched on the bedside lamp and picked up the topmost magazine, hoping to find its contents dull enough to induce drowsiness. It was a week-old copy of *Life* whose cover was a reproduction of Pieter Bruegel's *Tower of Babel* and whose teaser caption read: "The Great Peasant Hits the Road." There was a lengthy story together with twelve pages of photographs, timed to coincide with the opening of the collection's U.S. tour in the capital. He recalled that George Upp had attended the gala event at the National Gallery the same evening of their somewhat stormy meeting—or had been dragged to it by his wife. He decided that the article might provide the sedative he sought.

The exhibit represented a cooperative effort on the part of a score of museums and private collectors. It was the first —and possibly the last—time that such a large number of the works of the Flemish master had been brought together. Since Bruegel's output had been small and of this only about forty paintings survived, the collection comprised perhaps eighty per cent of the total. Every canvas was considered priceless. If you were to accept the value put on each (Duffy found it difficult), the total exhibit was undoubtedly the most awe-inspiring ever assembled. He was pleased to find his eyelids growing heavy; he read on.

The scheduled cross-country tour was so brief that it scarcely seemed to justify the years of negotiations and planning which had gone into it. Following the premiere in Washington, D.C., the paintings were to be displayed in only three other American cities—Los Angeles, Chicago and New York—before being returned to their owners. Reading the itinerary, Duffy realized that the tour had already reached the halfway point; the exhibit opened in Los Angeles tomorrow. Might drop by and see it, he thought, knowing that he would not. The article went on to detail the difficulties inherent in transporting and guarding the collection, as well as the well-nigh staggering cost of insuring it. For that reason, the carefully crated masterpieces were being conveyed exclusively by train.

The word jolted him fully awake. A cargo worth millions, proceeding on a schedule announced months in advance, and by train . . . He continued to read, feverishly now, seeking other evidence that would substantiate an almost incredible theory.

He found it on the final page. It was a half-column cut of a Dr. Leslie Rhyne, assistant curator of New York's Staufenberg Gallery. The accompanying text described Dr. Rhyne, a woman despite the somewhat masculine name, as the principal architect of the unique exhibit and supervisor of its American tour. Duffy stared at the surprisingly attractive, although somewhat austere, face for a long time. Photographs were often deceiving . . . but Dr. Leslie Rhyne bore a striking resemblance to the bad-mannered young woman he had encountered leaving the offices of Forte Enterprises, Inc.

Anthony Heaston awoke and knew, without confirmation from his wrist watch, that it was six A.M. The training of a lifetime roused him punctually each morning at the hour he willed. And, furthermore, refreshed no matter what time he had turned in the previous evening. The ability to control his sleep, not merely its duration but its quality, was an invaluable asset to a guerrilla. Success—and often survival—depended on such self-discipline.

He did not rise immediately but lay quietly while his mind reviewed the situation, another discipline. He tackled the assessment as systematically as a regimental morning report. Status of forces: unchanged. Level of training: excellent. Combat readiness: superior. Morale: satisfactory. "Satisfactory" was the military equivalent of damning with faint praise yet he could not honestly rate his men's mental attitude any higher. An army's morale was an intangible factor. Nothing eroded it more than marking time. His army was trained and ready. The best that he could promise them—and himself—was that the battle would be joined shortly, if last evening's news reports were accurate.

His thoughts turned to his enemy. Where was Duffy this morning? Lifting of the electronic surveillance would seem to indicate that he had given up the contest, yet Heaston detected in the younger man something of himself, the near mania that rendered defeat unacceptable. Heaston had won the first skirmish as regards the listening device. Perhaps he had won the second—Mindy's letter—also. However, he felt certain that their war was not over. Duffy commanded larger forces and superior firepower. Heaston had the greater experience and the advantage of surprise. The latter might prove to be the decisive factor. Unless Duffy had a crystal ball, Heaston did not see how he could figure out when and where the attack would take place—when Heaston himself did not yet know precisely.

Bronko stuck his head in the door while he was shaving. "Willie's back. Got in after midnight. I didn't wake you, thought his report could wait till morning."

"Call a formation," Heaston ordered, delighted at the news. He was about to learn where.

They gathered around the table, their exhilaration in marked contrast to the somberness which had characterized their council of war a few evenings previously. Only the newcomer showed no gaiety. Willie Votaw's cold, which Duffy had seen in infancy, had now reached maturity. Its host acknowledged their ribald greetings glumly.

"I got a headache that won't quit. So shut up and listen, 'cause I'm not about to repeat it."

Chastened, they clustered around while he spread a large map on the table and placed the transparent overlay on a portion of it. "There she is."

"What's all that writing mean?" Moby Dick wondered, pointing at the grease pencil notations.

"I'll go into that later," Votaw said wearily. "Right now all that matters is that we're in business. I've been over every inch of the line and this here's the only spot that fits all the specifications." He paused to wipe his nose. "First, the terrain is right. It's rugged country, mostly uninhabited and the railroad right-of-way doesn't lie close to any major highway. We can count on plenty of privacy. Second, you've got a division point here"—he tapped the map—"meaning our train will stop to pick up a fresh crew before heading into the target zone. That'll give us a chance to do what we have to do and make any last-minute adjustments in case they're running fast or slow."

"Is there any possibility that this particular train—considering its cargo—might not stop at the division point?"

"No way, Colonel. Union regulations say that crews change at each and every division point and not even God Almighty can bend that."

"Just checking. You know how important it is."

"Reckon I should if anyone does." Votaw sniffled.

"Third, the schedule calls for it to hit this particular stretch at night. There's another spot down here that checks out pretty good, too, but we couldn't count on darkness if they should be running late. Fourth and last, the place I picked is close enough to the advance base without being too close. Fifty miles as the crow flies, give or take a few. By the way, the last thing I did before heading back here was to check it out personally. Wouldn't be surprised that was where I caught my cold."

"What about the advance base?" Bronko prompted impatiently. "How does it stack up?"

"Everything's just the way Mr. Zeus said it was." Votaw became aware of their sudden silence. He looked from face to face, puzzled. "What's wrong?"

"Nothing, really," Heaston assured him. "We'd gotten in the habit of not mentioning that name, especially here. We had visitors while you were away, Willie. The law. They left a bug behind."

"How'd the fuzz ever get onto us? I've been so damn careful myself, wouldn't even carry the map and the overlay together just so's nobody could make a connection. Why'd you let me talk like this, anyway?"

"We fed the bug what we wanted the cops to hear and then we deactivated it. Nobody's listening to us now."

"Not even Mindy," Hack added with a glance at Bronko. "Might say we deactivated her, too."

"Mindy?" Votaw repeated. "Who the hell's that?"

Bronko uttered a short laugh. "Good question. Who the hell's that?"

The Los Angeles County Museum of Art on Wilshire Boulevard occupies a portion of what is properly named Hancock Park and is more commonly known as the La Brea Tarpits. For years it was a magnet for tourists who came to view the fossilized skeletons and concrete reproductions of the extinct creatures who once drank from the prehistoric watering hole and, frequently, died there. With the construction of the museum, art vied with paleontology as the park's principal attraction.

On this particular morning, art was clearly winning. The well-publicized arrival of the touring Bruegel collection had drawn a crowd numbering in the thousands. Duffy had difficulty finding a place to park or even to stand. The upper and lower plazas were jammed, as were the broad Y-shaped stairs which led from one to the other. Children perched precariously on the massive sculpture, despite efforts of museum attendants to prevent them, and some splashed delightedly in the shallow reflecting pool.

Once inside the gallery, he was not permitted to linger. Security was handled by a private police agency which kept the visitors moving steadily through a labyrinth of velvet ropes that put them within viewing—but not touching—distance of each painting. The thrust of the crowd made leisurely inspection impossible. The entire tour, from entrance to exit, was accomplished in less than thirty minutes. Since most of the spectators wished merely to be able to boast that they had glimpsed the masterpieces, there was little grumbling at the brevity of the glimpse. The unsatisfied minority joined the lines outside for a second look.

Duffy made the circuit three times before he saw what he had come to see, not the paintings but their guardian. Dr. Leslie Rhyne was shepherding a little flock of civic dignitaries and a larger herd of representatives from the news media on a privileged inspection which ignored the restraints placed on lesser mortals. Though the youngest of the group, she was plainly in control of it, answering their questions authoritatively and posing the officials with the paintings for the benefit of the photographers with the efficiency of a drillmaster.

She passed Duffy without seeing him. She was smiling this morning and her chestnut hair was fashioned into a long flowing ponytail instead of a bun, but there was no doubt that Leslie Rhyne was, indeed, the woman he had encountered at Forte Enterprises. Once again her handsome face was innocent of make-up and, once again, she wore the pants suit that appeared to be her uniform, although this time it was in a shade that matched the blue of her eyes.

Duffy dropped the notebook he carried and knelt to retrieve it. When he arose, he was on the other side of the velvet rope. He joined the squad of reporters, none of whom noticed the addition to their ranks. He did not call attention to himself by joining in their questions, many of which were repetitious and, in some cases, bordered on the puerile. He suspected that Leslie Rhyne felt the same way. However, she answered each courteously and patiently. Yes, this was the first time that such a representative collection of Bruegel's work had been available for general viewing. No, she would not attempt to place a price tag on it. The exhibit was insured for fifty million dollars, but this, of course, did not represent its true value. Yes, this would be the collection's only display west of the Mississippi and, no, she could not say precisely how long it would remain in Los Angeles. As previously announced, the schedule allowed a few days' flexibility, depending upon public response.

Only once did the temper which Duffy remembered seem to flare. That was in response to a suggestion that she tell them something of herself "for the woman's angle."

"There is no 'woman's angle,' " Leslie replied crisply. "I'm here in a professional capacity. Neither my personal life nor my gender is relevant."

"But isn't it unusual for a woman to be given such a big responsibility?" the reporter persisted.

Leslie eyed him coldly. "Women are used to big responsibilities. If you don't believe me, ask your mother."

The sarcasm won a laugh in which she did not join and put an end to that line of questioning. She also refused to pose with the paintings—"Bruegel can stand alone; he doesn't need cheesecake to help him"—and, likewise, declined to film a television interview, pleading lack of time. How about this evening? Sorry, she had a previous engagement. On that note the group dissolved, Leslie going off to lunch with officials of the museum, Duffy and the newsmen departing to their automobiles.

Leslie Rhyne had refused to divulge her life story to the reporters. Duffy sought it elsewhere. He spent the afternoon at the public library, delving into reference books and magazines of limited circulation. From them, he learned that she had been born twenty-nine years earlier at Chicopee Falls, Massachusetts. Her widowed mother—also a Dr. Rhyne—still resided there and taught psychology at Mount Holyoke College. Leslie, an only child and a precocious one, had received her B.A. from that institution with honors in art, her master's from Smith and her doctorate from Harvard. She had joined the Staufenberg Gallery, risen rapidly to the post of assistant curator and was recognized as a leading authority on the Flemish painters. She had written several articles on Bruegel and was quoted in articles written by others. She was unmarried. Her address in Manhattan was in a section Duffy recognized as a neighborhood of modestly priced apartments.

Altogether a pretty high-powered dame, he decided, a rare combination of beauty, brains and—he felt sure, from personal observation as well as the dossier—guts. It took all three to make it in a man's world and Leslie was obviously making it. However, that was only an outsider's view. She might have an entirely opposite opinion. He did not know what an assistant curator earned—he guessed the salary wasn't spectacular—and perhaps Leslie had devised a plan to achieve the financial rewards her education and ability deserved. It seemed bizarre but there was no denying that she, architect and custodian of the priceless collection, had some connection with Forte Enterprises which had leased the Tres Muertos ranch to Anthony Heaston's HH Company. Her involvement, and Forte's, might only be innocently peripheral, nothing more than a coincidence. But Duffy, like all lawmen, was made uneasy by coincidences.

The doors to the gallery closed at six P.M. Duffy returned to the museum shortly before the hour and parked his automobile (not his, actually, but Selena's) where he might observe the exit. An hour passed before Leslie appeared. She came down the broad steps and strode across the plaza directly toward him, waving a hand as if in greeting. He was relieved to discover that the gesture was not meant for him but for a cruising taxi.

The chase was short, terminating at a large coffee shop. By the time he parked and went inside, Leslie was already seated in a booth for two. He chose another a short distance behind her. From the way she kept glancing at her wrist watch, he wondered if she expected someone to join her. No one did; both the woman and her pursuer supped alone. Duffy left first, to be in position to take up the pursuit once more.

This time it was considerably longer. Leslie engaged a second cab which carried her the length of Wilshire Boulevard, through Beverly Hills and Westwood and Santa Monica to Venice. Duffy, trailing close behind, grew more puzzled with every mile. He did not know whether the appointment Leslie had pleaded involved business or pleasure. However, the seaside suburb was not one where out-of-state visitors normally sought either.

His bewilderment increased when he learned her destination—a shabby two-story office building in a section devoted to warehouses and light industries. Leslie paid the cabbie and refused his offer to wait. Duffy, parked a half block away, watched her enter the building.

The concrete block structure, fully a half-century old and looking every year of it, boasted neither lobby nor elevator. There was a directory at the foot of the stairs, but it was badly out of date. Those names which had not been crossed out—marginal businesses for the most part—gave no clue as to which a Ph.D. in art might be expected to visit. The offices on the street level were dark. Duffy climbed the dusty stairs which were illuminated by a single naked light bulb.

The upper level offered more possibilities. Light seeped from beneath two of the doors. He discarded the first since it was marked *Women* and approached the second cautiously. There was no keyhole through which to peer but, by placing his ear against the panel, he could distinguish the murmur of voices although not the words.

His concentration was abruptly broken by words he could hear all too well. They came not from the room beyond the door but from the corridor behind him. "What are you doing there!"

Duffy spun about, startled, to discover a young woman staring at him. She was a diminutive creature, barely out of her teens, with brown hair plaited into braids. She was clad in coarse white cotton slacks and a floppy tunic of the same color and fabric. Her bare feet accounted for his failure to notice her approach.

There was no time for an explanation even if he had been prepared with one. He grabbed for her waist and her mouth, hoping to stifle the scream that would betray him. The girl had no intention of screaming—or of being seized. She, not he, did the seizing. Duffy found himself flying through the air, a flight which ended abruptly as he collided with the wall. The crash seemed to rock the ancient building to its foundations.

It came to him tardily what he should have recognized immediately—that the loose-fitting costume was that customarily worn by students of judo. Young and tiny though she might be, the girl was no novice. Employing his momentum to full advantage, she had flipped him over her hip in a near classic demonstration of the Oriental art. Duffy was in no position to compliment her upon her skill—or, in fact, to do anything at all. His arms were twisted painfully behind his back while a bare foot on his neck pressed his face into the grime of the corridor.

Stunned as much by surprise as by the fall, he became aware of a babble of voices. He saw by turning his eyes to the side that he was surrounded by other feet, some of them bare and all of them female. The commotion had drawn forth the occupants of the room.

He recognized Leslie's crisp tones. "What happened, Marci? Who is this?"

"I don't know," his conqueror replied. "I found him listening at the door. He tried to grab me and, well . . . What should I do with him?"

"Let him sit up." Duffy got gratefully to his knees, shaking his head to clear it. But when he would have risen farther, Leslie snapped, "I said sit, not stand. Stay right there while we get a look at you. Anyone recognize this—this gentleman?"

There was a murmur from the circle of hostile faces disclaiming prior acquaintanceship. "Perhaps I do," Leslie said, bending closer to peer into their captive's face. "This morning—at the museum. He was one of the reporters."

The announcement, far from absolving him, reacted on the group as unfavorably as if he had been identified as a cobra. A majority drew back with loathing and alarm while a smaller number appeared ready to destroy him.

"That's right, isn't it? You're here to spy on us so you can write another one of your snide, sneering oh-so-amusing stories about the Women's Liberation Front."

"Women's Liberation Front?" Duffy echoed in a choked voice. "Female equality, rights for women . . . Is that you are?"

"Oh, come off it! You know very well who we are. I'll thank you not to play dumb."

"Who's playing?" He summoned up a weak grin. "I'm not a reporter. Much as it embarrasses me to admit it, I'm a special investigator for the FBI. You know—those dauntless champions of justice, the terrors of the underworld. Now would you ladies please allow me to get up?"

He gave Leslie Rhyne a ride back into the city. "I'm really sorry Marci roughed you up," she told him. "I don't approve of violence. I wouldn't want you to think it's part of our program."

"I won't tell if you won't."

"Of course, what happened tonight is understandable. Women's Lib has been so ridiculed by your male-dominated press, our aims so distorted, that we've practically been driven underground. Why, reporters have used every dirty trick from seduction to dressing in drag just so they could get their stories, the whole purpose of which is to make us look like freaks."

"How did a pretty girl like you mixed up in this, anyway?"

"You might say I was born into it. I suppose being named Leslie helped, too. After years of being put down by male professors and employers with 'Sorry, I thought from your name that you were a man' . . . Well, it does get under one's skin. So does your question, by the way. What does my being pretty have to do with anything?"

"I meant it as a compliment."

"But a patronizing one. You'd resent it if I asked what a handsome boy like you is doing playing policeman, wouldn't you?"

"Maybe it was patronizing, at that," Duffy conceded. "You'll have to forgive me. I guess I'm not used to the New Woman."

"You mean you're not used to an honest woman. We've Uncle Tommed it for so long, pretending to be weaker and dumber to build up your egos—gaining security by selling our self-respect along with our bodies—telling lies like 'I'm sorry, darling, but I have a simply splitting headache' when what we really mean is 'Not until I want it, too' . . . Well, the times they are a-changing, Mr. Duffy. Women deserve equality and we mean to have it."

"I'm all for equality—but do you really believe that burning your bras is the way to achieve it?"

"That's just a symbolic action—like dumping tea in Boston harbor. Every revolution needs to dramatize itself. If burning our bras makes you sit up and take notice, I say burn 'em."

"I'll be interested to see how your revolution makes out."

"Are you speaking personally or professionally? You still haven't explained why you are following me. Has Women's

Lib made the FBI's subversive list?"

"Oh, you're a subversive group, all right, but you don't come under our jurisdiction. The reason I got on your trail was that I had the wild notion that you were fixing to rob a train."

"You're kidding!" Leslie exclaimed incredulously. "No, I can see you're not. Would you mind telling me why?"

Duffy declined, not merely because the information was confidential but because now that he knew more of Leslie Rhyne, his theory—insofar as it concerned her—sounded too ridiculous to bear repeating. "Sorry, but I can't discuss the case." He added with a grin, "I'd tell a man the same thing. All I can say is that my investigation involves Forte Enterprises. At least, I thought it did. And since I bumped into you there—"

"When?" Even after he had refreshed her memory, she could not recall the incident. "I must have made a terrible impression on you. I apologize. I remember I was furious. That's no excuse, of course, but after the way that man led me on for nearly a year—"

"Niblo? Why, that old goat!"

"Oh, not Mr. Niblo. He's a perfect dear. I mean Julian Loud. You know that he is Forte Enterprises, don't you?"

"I didn't. I guess I should have. Forte—Loud. Of course."

"Well, it just so happens that Julian Loud owns the largest private collection of Bruegels in the world. I worked for months through Mr. Niblo, trying to get him to agree to let us include his paintings in our exhibit. I thought I nearly had him convinced, too. I even made a special trip out here to get his answer. I got it, all right, a flat no. He didn't even have the graciousness to say sorry."

"From what I hear, that's par for the course."

"But what sort of a person can he be, not even to give an

explanation? Mr. Niblo—he felt nearly as badly as I did about it—sort of hinted that Loud was afraid that if he put the paintings on display, the rightful owners might claim them. The Nazis looted the Dutch museums during the war. Several Bruegels disappeared. Those may be what Loud has. That's just a guess, because no one's actually seen his collection. I prefer to believe that the real reason Julian Loud turned me down is that he's a rotten fink." She noticed his smile and said defensively, "Well, he is, you know. What has he ever done with all those billions except pander to his ego? Women, paintings, property—whatever he wants he gets, never mind who gets hurt in the process."

"I expect that, underneath, he's really miserable."

"I wish I thought so, but I don't. I think he thoroughly enjoys playing God. I'm sure that's how he sees himself. After all, look at that alias he uses. Mr. Zeus! Any man who'd call himself—"

She broke off with a gasp of alarm as the automobile swerved suddenly toward the curb. "Sorry," Duffy muttered, getting the vehicle under control. "What was that again? Loud uses the name of Mr. Zeus?"

"Whenever he travels incognito—which is about the only way he ever does travel. If you remember your Greek mythology, Zeus frequently liked to slip down from Mount Olympus and meddle with human affairs for his own amusement."

"Tell me more. You say he has a passion for Bruegel? Loud—not Zeus."

"Mania is a better word. Not only does he have the largest private collection of Bruegel's paintings, but he's tried for years to get his hands on the rest. Some of the offers he's made you wouldn't believe. Why, there's even a rumor that he hired some men to try to steal *Mad Meg* from the

Rotterdam Museum." She added reluctantly, "I don't really believe that, it's simply too fantastic. Not even Julian Loud would go that far."

"Fantastic is the word for it, all right. But then you might say it's a fantastic world."

"Turn right at the next signal," Leslie directed. "I'm in the middle of the second block." She was staying not in a hotel but in a nearby apartment provided courtesy of the museum. Duffy walked her to the door. "Would you like to come in?"

"Dare I inquire what for?"

"Nothing—or everything, it all depends," she told him candidly. "I'm lonely and I like you. We can start from there."

"I'd love to, but I'm afraid I can't, not tonight." He grinned. "Would you believe that I have a simply splitting headache?"

Raymond was furious, and not merely because the telephone had roused him from his bed; it was one A.M. in Washington.

"Am I glad to hear from you!" he informed Duffy in a tone which contradicted the sentiment. "I was afraid I wasn't going to have the pleasure of telling you exactly what I think of you." He launched into a description of his subordinate's heredity, habits and prospects which—had it been addressed to a stranger—could have been classified as an obscene call.

"Calm down, F.X.," Duffy advised when he paused for breath.

"I have calmed down! You should have heard me yesterday!"

The indictment was disobedience to orders; Raymond spit out the bill of particulars. The Denver Mint, in a routine checkback, had inquired if the Jacob Duffy who had interrogated the superintendant regarding the Mint's systems and procedures was actually the FBI agent he claimed to be. Immediately afterward, Raymond had received a second call, this one from Paul Collins, the agent-in-charge of the Los Angeles office. The airline had complained to Collins over FBI interference with their baggage operations and Collins angrily demanded to know why Duffy was poaching in his territory. Raymond could only conclude that Duffy, far from vacationing in Florida, was continuing his investigation of the Heaston matter—which added up to a flagrant case of insubordination.

Duffy realized that Raymond, despite his wrath, still hoped that his protégé might justify his conduct. "You're absolutely right, F.X. I've behaved outrageously."

"Apologies won't help. Can you give me one single solitary reason I shouldn't fire you?"

"How will this do? I've found out what Heaston intends to steal, how he intends to steal it and who's behind him. By tomorrow I expect to know where and when, too."

There was silence at the other end of the line. When Raymond finally spoke, his anger had been replaced by cautious interest. "Tell me more."

"I'd rather not go into details over the phone. This needs to be talked out face to face. Since I can't come there, I was hoping you'd come here."

"I guess that could be arranged. I'll have to check on what flight's available."

"There's one leaving Dulles at six A.M. your time. You should be able to get a seat."

Raymond grunted. "You mean you haven't already made my reservation? Okay, Jake, meet me at the airport."

"One more thing, F.X. Better leave word with your secretary to tear up those charges against me."

"Not a chance," Raymond growled. "But I will tell her to put them in my Hold basket—just in case."

Duffy had used the telephone in his cousin's den to make the call. Now he used the liquor in his cousin's bar to fix himself a drink. He downed it with a sense of elation. His shoulder throbbed from its collision with the wall, but a bruise was a small price to pay for the knowledge it had gained him. Whistling (softly, so as not to disturb his hosts, who had already retired), he went up the stairs to his bedroom. Before retiring, he'd take another look at the handkerchief on which he'd traced the symbols and numerals from the plastic overlay, see if he couldn't . . .

To his surprise, it was not on the dresser where he had placed it. His elation turned suddenly to dismay. Selena—bless her thoughtful little heart!—had taken advantage of his absence to wash his dirty clothing. The precious handkerchief sat atop the stack of clean underwear, laundered and pressed and as free of stains as the day he had purchased it.

Raymond arrived the next morning—almost, he pointed out, before he had left, thanks to the speed of jet travel and the leapfrogging of three time zones. Duffy drove him into the smog-covered city, postponing discussion with the excuse, "There's someone I want you to meet first."

The crowd at their destination caused Raymond to raise his bushy white eyebrows. "You didn't tell me you were holding a reception in my honor."

"I remembered how you love surprises, F.X. Anyway, some of these people may have come to see the Bruegel exhibit."

He had made arrangements through Leslie to use the Museum of Art's parking lot. She met them at the gallery's private entrance in the rear and escorted them to the office which had been placed at her disposal.

"Get over your headache?" she asked slyly and explained to Raymond, "Poor Jake had a bit of a fight last night."

"You promised you wouldn't tell."

Raymond groaned. "I hope you didn't kill anybody."

"Oh, no. Jake was very merciful."

"Suppose we get down to business," Duffy suggested uncomfortably. "F.X. already had a pretty good idea what our business amounts to but you don't, Leslie, so I'll start from the beginning." He spoke deliberately and at length, omitting nothing, from the suspicions of the ailing ex-President which had launched the investigation, through the evidence that investigation had produced, to the conclusions he had drawn from it.

"Incredible," Raymond muttered when he had finished. "I don't say it can't be true, but it's still incredible that a man like Julian Loud—"

"Loud has a passion for Bruegel—Leslie calls it a mania—and Loud has made a career out of indulging his passions. What he wants, he usually gets, one way or another, legally or illegally. We know he wants the Bruegels. He's made some fantastic bids for the paintings. There's even a rumor he tried to have one heisted."

"That's never been proved," Leslie pointed out.

"Doesn't matter. The fact that the rumor even exists, that it wasn't laughed to death years ago, shows that Loud is known to be a man who's capable of anything. He's a law unto himself. Since he hasn't been able to buy the Bruegels, why not steal them? Your American tour—the first and probably the last time the paintings have ever been assembled in a single exhibit—gives him a once-in-a-lifetime opportunity."

Leslie remained as incredulous as Raymond, but for a different reason. "I'm certainly willing to believe the worst of Julian Loud. What I can't believe is that he'd risk so much on such an impossible scheme."

"What's Loud actually risking except maybe a couple hundred thousand bucks? He can spare that out of petty cash. You can bet that he isn't personally involved. If the holdup flops, Heaston and his Hellions take the rap and Julian Loud never heard of them. Or if he needs another scapegoat there's always Ira Niblo, who's too scared of the boss to understand what's going on under his nose." Duffy shrugged. "As far as the scheme being impossible, I couldn't agree less. Dangerous, yes. Risky, sure. But impossible? Not at all. The reason is that nobody really believes a train can be robbed these days. Case in point. How many guards do you have watching the Bruegels right now, Leslie?"

"Three eight-man shifts around the clock. Twenty-four men in all."

"And how many guards do you have aboard the train?"

"Four," she admitted ruefully. "I see what you mean."

"Everyone including the insurance companies—who have the tables to back them up—considers the train ride the safest part of the journey so far as theft is concerned. It's take-off-the-shoes-and-put-up-the-feet time. The unguarded moment is what every good thief dreams of. And every good guerrilla too, I'll bet."

"So Heaston pulls the heist and the paintings vanish into Julian Loud's underground collection, never to be seen again," Raymond mused. "It does begin to add up. Okay, Jake, you've told us the how and the why of it. You also promised the when and where."

"The when is easy. Sometime within thirty-six hours after the collection heads out of L.A. for Chicago. I'm convinced that Heaston means to hit the train before it crosses the Mississippi. As to the where . . . I thought I'd know that by now, but it turns out I don't." He described the plastic overlay he had found in Willie Votaw's suitcase and how he had transcribed its notations onto his handkerchief, only to have them erased by Selena Spydell's well-meant labors.

Raymond could not repress his laughter. Duffy did not share his superior's amusement. Neither did Leslie. "But what are you going to do, Jake?"

"Reconstruct it from memory if I can. Do without it if I can't."

"No, I mean how are you going to stop them from robbing the train?"

"Why, I'm going to let them rob the train, naturally." He grinned at her shocked expression. "Except that it'll be the wrong train. The exhibit will continue here as per schedule. Comes time to leave, you'll announce for all the world to hear how nice it's been and you're on your merry way back east. When Anthony Heaston sticks up the train somewhere between here and there, he'll learn to his immense chagrin that it's loaded with special agents instead of priceless paintings."

"But why take the risk of something going wrong? Why not simply arrest Heaston and his gang now?"

"No proof. Got to catch 'em in the act. Also, there's the future to consider. Heaston's Hellions are a pretty hairy bunch, always were. Now that Julian Loud has put them back in business, they may decide to stay there. No telling what mischief they might think up next time."

Leslie sighed. "You seem to have it all figured out."

"No, I don't have it all figured out—not quite. There's still one piece missing. Why Heaston?"

"I don't understand what you mean."

"Why did Loud choose Anthony Heaston to steal the Bruegels? He certainly could have found other men just as willing and with a lot more experience—yet he went to all the trouble of busting Heaston out of the Colombian prison. There's got to be a reason. It bothers me that I haven't been able to come up with it."

"Maybe you're too close to the trees to see the forest," Raymond suggested. "I can think of a couple of good reasons for Loud picking Heaston. One, that he didn't want to use underworld talent because they have a habit of shooting off their mouths. Two, robbing a train is practically a military operation. It calls for an army, not a gang. Who's better qualified to lead an army that Mad Anthony Heaston?"

"I guess it doesn't really matter much, anyway. I'd just be happier knowing for sure."

"You can ask Heaston when you catch him." Raymond rose briskly. "That's your job, Jake. I'd gladly trade it for mine. I've got to break the news to George Upp that the Heaston case isn't closed, after all. I expect he'll roar like a bull elephant when he hears you went against his orders."

"He should be grateful Jake did," Leslie said. "I know I am."

"One thing you must never expect when you disobey a general, and that's gratitude. The best Jake will get from Upp is a pardon, given very, very grudgingly—and that only if he pulls the thing off." He placed a warning hand on Duffy's shoulder. "For that reason, laddie, if for no other, don't blow it."

Clyde Munn looked to be exactly what he was—a cop. It was not so much a case of size (although Munn was a large man) or muscles (with which he was generously supplied) but rather an aura which all veteran lawmen seem to acquire—a self-assured forcefulness manifested in both speech and bearing. It begins as a posture; it ends as a characteristic. Munn possessed a full measure of it. Yet he was no ordinary cop but the chief security officer for the Association of Western Rail Carriers, the top policemen for the twelve major railroads which composed the Association.

His office was located close by the Union Depot in downtown Los Angeles. However, he invited Duffy to meet him not where he worked but where he played, at the YMCA. Munn was on the handball courts when he arrived.

Although past fifty, Munn held a national ranking in the strenuous sport. It was easy to see why. He took up a position near mid-court from which he seldom seemed to move and from which he ran his much younger opponent into exhaustion and eventual collapse. The final score was 21–3; Munn made the victory look easy.

Duffy followed him to the locker room and amused himself with the punching bag while Munn showered. "I don't usually schedule meetings here," Munn apologized. "But I couldn't default the match without dropping out of the tournament and I'm catching a plane to Spokane at one-thirty, and since you said your business couldn't wait . . ."

"Is there someplace around here we can talk privately?"

"Guess Chuck wouldn't mind if we borrowed his office while he's out to lunch." Munn led him into the glass-enclosed cubicle which belonged to the athletic director and sat on the desk to lace his shoes. "Okay, shoot. What's the FBI up to now?"

Duffy told him, omitting the details which did not concern the other man and elaborating on those which did. Munn listened with the air of one who found nothing unbelievable, no matter how bizarre. "Hasn't been a decent train robbery in years," he commented. "Just penny ante stuff—packages, mail sacks, that sort of thing. Best one I can remember was a boxcar full of television sets and we caught them before they got it unloaded. Always thought I'd like a crack at something really big. How many of my men are you going to need?"

"None." Duffy smiled at his disappointment. "I've already got enough manpower. You can help me in other ways—first, by telling me what you make of this."

Munn studied the sheet of paper on which he had placed, as accurately as memory allowed, the symbols and numerals from the plastic overlay. "Doesn't mean a thing to me." And even after Duffy had explained its significance, he continued to shake his head. "Without the map it goes to, it's worthless."

"I want you to find the map. You must have a complete collection."

"Sure, I got the maps—but they cover over one hundred thousand miles of track."

"It isn't really that big a job. We can eliminate everything except the Santa Fe system, because that's the only one our train will use."

"That's still close to ten thousand miles. Even if we had the original overlay, which we don't, and even if your sketch is accurate, which it probably isn't, there's no way of pinpointing the stretch it's supposed to cover. Maps come in all sizes, Duffy. We don't know the scale of the original. We don't have any reference points. We don't even have compass directions. All we do have are a few X's and O's and a flock of numbers."

"That should be enough for us to make some educated guesses."

"Go ahead," Munn growled. "Dazzle me with your brilliance."

"Forget the X's and O's, because they could stand for anything. But take the numerals. Look at how they're written. 90—1:15. 110—1:37. I think that the first figure represents mileage between two points, the second set the time it takes the train to cover the distance. The arrows from the numerals must point to the track. It's true that we don't know the scale of the original. But every map, no matter what its scale, is laid out with north at the top and south at the bottom. The way the arrows almost form steps, I'd say that the stretch of track we want runs southwest to northeast. Are we getting warmer?"

"Maybe." Munn squinted as if trying to visualize the tracks which spanned two-thirds of a continent. "You can throw out most of Arizona and all of Kansas. That still leaves Caifornia, New Mexico, Colorado and parts of Oklahoma and Texas." He grimaced. "Looks like I've got my work cut out for me. How much time do we have?"

"The paintings are due in Chicago on the fifteenth. That means they can't depart L.A. later than Thursday. Since the dummy shipment has to go first to clear the track, that leaves us three and a half days, four at the outside."

"I'll give it my best shot," Munn promised. "Can I keep this paper?"

"It's yours. But please—don't put it with your dirty clothes."

There was an extra being hawked on the streets as he went to reclaim his automobile from the parking lot. He strained to decipher the newsboy's shouts but failed. Curious, since an extra in this era of instantaneous electronic communication was a rarity, he turned on the radio to seek a news broadcast. The dial contained nothing else. Orrin Kell Carson, General of the Armies and former President of the United States, had died at Walter Reed Hospital in the nation's capital. Messages of sympathy were pouring in from governments and prominent figures around the globe; a national month of mourning had been proclaimed in honor of the old hero.

The news, while not unexpected, saddened him as it did most who heard it although he, like they, had known Carson only from a distance. Nevertheless, O.K. had been a part of his life for as long as he could remember. His passing seemed to make the world a little emptier. Duffy felt a secondary regret that no other mourner shared. It was O.K. Carson who had sent him out to do battle with Anthony Heaston and who now would never know of his victory.

Raymond thought that George Upp had aged ten years since their last meeting. Upp acknowledged the unspoken opinion. "Nothing like the death of an old comrade to make you realize you're not a youngster any more," he said wearily. Called to the hospital when death appeared imminent, he had spent the hours since consoling the widow in the dual capacity of long-time friend and Presidential representative. Although it was now nearly midnight, his duties were not yet over. Arthur Carson and his wife were flying home from his ambassadorial post in Europe. Upp had been delegated to meet the plane. Raymond rode with him to the airport.

"I'm just thankful the funeral arrangements were made in advance," Upp replied to his commiserations. "I doubt if I'd be up to handling them, too."

Yet even an ill wind blows someone good; Upp was too exhausted to react to Raymond's report with the indignation it would have aroused at another time. Even Duffy's insubordination didn't produce the expected explosion.

He was not too fatigued to express an opinion, however. "If I had to sum it up in one word, that word would be hogwash! I refuse to believe that someone of the stature of Julian Loud would stoop to stealing a bunch of old pictures. I saw the exhibit myself, F.X. I wouldn't give you ten bucks for the whole lot."

"One man's trash is another man's treasure, as they say."

"I suppose. All right, what's your next move? Arrest Heaston and his cutthroats, I suppose."

"We've got to let Heaston make his move first. Otherwise, we don't have a case."

Upp's authoritarian background made him impatient with such niceties. "I say arrest Heaston now, sweat the truth out of him. Then you'll have your case."

"And if Heaston won't sweat—what then?"

"Well, at the very least, you'll have stopped him from robbing any trains. Or whatever."

"Are we willing to pay the price?" Raymond asked quietly. "If we jail Heaston on a charge we can't possibly make stick, we've protected the Bruegels, sure. But at the same time we make Heaston look like a victim of unjust persecution. The press will certainly dredge up the Do Binh scandal which I understood the Administration would prefer forgotten. Not only is there an election coming but at this particular moment, with General Carson's funeral and all . . . Of course, if you want me to order Duffy to stop—"

"What guarantee could you give me that he would?" Which proved that Duffy's disobedience had not entirely escaped Upp's notice, after all. "You're right about the bad publicity," he said in a grudging voice. "But what kind of a press do you think we'd get if Heaston should manage to pull off his holdup and it came out—as it would—that we'd known about it in advance?"

"There's an element of risk in everything, even crossing the street," Raymond admitted. "But Heaston's walking into a trap. Duffy won't let him walk out of it. I'd stake my reputation on that."

"You are," Upp told him grimly. He sighed. "All right, F.X. Tell your young mastermind to proceed. But tell him also that if he fails, his is one funeral I'll be delighted to handle personally."

THREE

> Hub shot down the pike so goldarn fast,
> They couldn't be seen until they was past.
> Still that ol' sun was beginnin' to gain
>   On the iron known as The Gravy Train.
>
> The fireman said, "There's no use tryin',
> Don't mind sweatin' but do hate dyin',
> Throttle down now or we'll all be slain,
>   And ride to hell in The Gravy Train."
>
> But Hub gave the throttle one more crack,
> Till them steel wheels barely touched the track,
> Laughin' meanwhile like he'd gone insane,
>   And kept highballin' The Gravy Train.
>
>   —The Ballad of The Gravy Train

"Turning to the local scene: If you haven't yet seen the multimillion-dollar Bruegel exhibit at the county Museum of Art, better hurry! The unique collection of the works of the fifteenth-century Flemish master winds up its L.A. showing today and heads for Chicago tomorrow. Due to unprecedented public interest—which has already caused the tour to be held over an extra day—the museum announces that the doors will remain open until eight P.M. tonight.

"The city council today . . ."

The same, or a variant of it, could be heard on every radio station and television channel through Southern California. Remembering the constantly playing radio at Tres Muertos, Duffy felt sure that the message would reach those for whom it was primarily intended.

Duffy himself heard it in Clyde Munn's office. "I wanted to see that exhibit myself," Munn fretted. "You've kept me so busy I haven't had a chance. How is it, by the way?"

Duffy didn't look up from the map which covered most of the desk. "Personally, I find this a lot more fascinating."

"Would you like me to sign it for you?"

"I'll settle for an explanation."

The single long sheet of paper was not one map but three, placed together for easier reference. They represented the sections of track which corresponded roughly to the sketch Duffy had reconstructed from memory.

"Taking them from west to east," Munn said, "Map A is California, between San Bernardino and Barstow. B is Holbrook, Arizona, to Gallup, New Mexico. And C is Raton, New Mexico, to La Junta, Colorado. Sorry I can't put my finger on just one and say 'This is it,' but none of them fits exactly."

"My memory may not be exact, either."

"You said it, I didn't. If I had to choose, I'd go along with A, the Mojave Desert stretch. It matches your data as well as the others and it's closest to the Imperial Valley, where you say the gang is holed up."

Duffy studied the timetable for a few moments before shaking his head. "I don't think so, Clyde. It's closest to their base, all right. But the train pulls out of here at 8:07 A.M. That puts it in the Mojave a couple hours later. I can't see Heaston pulling the hijack in broad daylight. If I were he, I'd want the advantage of darkness."

"Wish you'd told me that to begin with. We could have

disregarded every section the train doesn't hit at night."

"No, we couldn't. I can't guarantee I'm right. A's a long-shot but still a possibility. B—the Arizona-New Mexico stretch—is a little better. We don't get into Gallup until after sunset. Of course, twilight and darkness aren't exactly the same thing."

"So what you're saying is that it's got to be C."

"It does strike me as the most likley. And I can't forget that Colorado was where I bumped into Willie Votaw."

"Then why not throw a ring around C, seal it off?"

"It'd take more manpower than I've got. And it might scare Heaston off. Nope, we'll figure that the hijack will take place at one of these locations, with C the most likely —and be ready for all three." Duffy tossed the timetable aside. "Now tell me about the train."

"It'll be the regularly scheduled highliner, Chicago via Kansas City, the way we agreed. Nothing unusual about it except that it'll pull four sleeping cars instead of three. I'm putting on an extra Pullman for you and your men. Thought that'd cause less suspicion than if we bumped passengers who already have their reservations. Should keep innocent bystanders out of the line of fire, too."

"Normal crew?"

"Uh-huh. They won't know there's anything different about this run. Oh, they will be told they're carrying the Bruegels, just in case anybody should ask. But they won't be told the crates are empty."

"I'll want a rundown on the other passengers, the so-called innocent bystanders. Heaston may be planning to put some of his men aboard."

"You'll have the complete list by the time you pull out. Shouldn't be hard to check. Passenger traffic isn't too heavy any more. With your men, this'll be the largest group we've hauled in a long time. How many do you expect to have, by the way?"

"Eighteen special agents, all from out of state. Adding you and me, that makes twenty. Or am I mistaken in assuming you want to go along?"

Munn grinned. "I was afraid you weren't going to ask. Since you have, I'll buy you dinner."

"Sorry, I'm already booked. Remembering what train food is like, I made sure of one decent meal before I left."

His date with Leslie was for nine o'clock. When he arrived punctually at her apartment, he was not surprised to find that she had still not dressed. He was surprised, however, to learn that she did not intend to.

"Would you mind if I fixed dinner for us here, Jake? I'm so tired of restaurants. Tonight I'd rather be domestic."

"Okay by me—but would Women's Lib approve?"

"All Women's Lib wants is equality. So we'll split the work. You set the table while I whip up a salad. Oh, and turn off that darn TV."

The real reason for her decision to dine in, she confessed, sprang less from a jaded appetite than a melancholy spirit. Prior to his arrival, she had been watching a recapitulation of the funeral of Orrin Kell Carson, held earlier in the nation's capital. The somber pageantry of the past several days—from the lying in state in the Capitol rotunda to the services in the National Cathedral—had been difficult to avoid. Regular programming was virtually suspended; the networks had done their usual job of saturation coverage, amounting almost to overkill.

"It's so depressing, really," Leslie sighed.

"Funerals usually are."

"This one was—oh, I don't know—especially hard to take. All those people filing past the casket, hour after hour. Then in the cathedral . . . the camera kept zooming in on their faces, and most of them were crying. He was a good man, Jake—not a great President, I guess—but a good man."

"Funny, I wouldn't have picked O.K. to be one of your heroes."

"He wasn't, not really. I did admire him, though. There was nothing petty or small about him. You should have seen his funeral, so simple and dignified and right . . . According to TV, he drew up the plans himself years ago to keep it from being turned into a circus. That's the mark of a real man, in my opinion. Most of them dump it all on the shoulders of their poor widows."

"On the other hand, O.K. had some pretty old-fashioned notions about women. Their proper place is in the home, that sort of thing."

"So did my father. That doesn't mean I didn't love him and respect him. Daddy and O.K. were a lot alike. I didn't necessarily agree with everything they stood for, but at least they stood for something!" She sighed. "I don't expect you to understand, especially on an empty stomach. How do you like your steak?"

"Delayed. I'd better check in with headquarters. I'm expecting a call. Paul may be paging me at Perino's right now."

Collins was not at his office. However, he had left a message for Duffy with the night supervisor.

"Good news?" Leslie asked, noting his smile.

"I think so. Earlier today, I asked the Border Patrol to check Tres Muertos with the excuse that they were looking for wetbacks. They report that Heaston and his men have cleared out, lock, stock and helicopter. That could mean only one of two things. Either they got tired of the resort business—or they're planning to stick up a certain train.

By this time tomorrow we should have a pretty good idea which."

Leslie paused in her labors to study him curiously. "Aren't you scared? I know I am."

Duffy frowned. "You don't have some crazy idea that you're going with me, do you?"

"I'm surprised you haven't suggested it yourself because you need me. That train is supposed to be carrying the Bruegels. I've been with them every step of the way. How's it going to look if I'm not aboard? You don't want Heaston to realize it's a trap."

"That's a chance I have to take. Getting you shot full of holes is a chance I don't have to take. And please skip that line about equal rights for women. It doesn't apply here."

"You don't have to shout."

"I'm not shouting. And you're not going."

"Well, of course, you're the boss. On the other hand, it may not be so very dangerous. When Colonel Heaston sees he's licked, he'll probably surrender meekly."

"He won't," Duffy declared flatly.

"What makes you so sure of that?"

"Because Heaston and I are a lot alike. Surrender means prison. He's gone that route once. If he feels the same way I did about it, he'd rather die than face it again."

Leslie blinked. "I don't understand. You've never been in prison."

"I spent nine months in the federal penitentiary at Atlanta. There was this Cosa Nostra soldier, a triggerman, whose testimony we needed to nail his boss. I was planted inside to work on him, convince him he'd been double-crossed by his 'family' so he'd be willing to sing. He broke before I did, but just between us it was a photo finish." He shuddered at the memory. "And that was only nine months, not ten to twenty years. I guarantee Heaston'll make a fight of it, to the death, probably."

"It must have been ghastly," she murmured. "Why did you ever agree to do it?"

"Matter of fact, it was my idea. There wasn't any other way to do the job."

"That's awfully important to you, isn't it, Jake? Not just doing your job but doing it better than anybody else. Even if it means going to prison—or disobeying orders like you did this time—you'll do anything to win, won't you?"

"That's the only way I know how to live."

"Then you make even less sense than I supposed. Here you are facing the biggest challenge of your life, one you'll do anything to win—and you're willing to risk losing rather than let me help you. And why? Simply because quote this is no place for a lady unquote. Admit it, Jake. The only thing you've got against me is my sex."

"Mostly, I guess," he admitted. "Come to think of it, that's what I've mostly got for you, too."

"Don't change the subject. Are you going to invite me to go with you or not?"

He surrendered with a sigh. "Okay, on the understanding that you obey my orders, you can come along. Surprised?"

"Completely."

"Good. I like to keep my women off balance. I'll help you pack after dinner."

"Oh, I packed before you got here, to save time." She stooped to peer into the broiler. "How did you say you like your steak? Rare, I hope."

"I really like mine medium. But something tells me that I'm going to get it rare anyhow."

In the marshaling yards in central Los Angeles, the process of putting together or—in railroadese—"making up" the train designated in the operating timetable as Number 437 had already begun. It could not yet properly be called a train, but merely fragments of one, and these fragments were widely separated.

In the huge service barns, crews labored to make ready the diesel-electric engines. There were three of the powerful monsters required to propel the streamliner on its swift journey across the continent, two A units and one B unit. The A units were larger, nearly seventy feet in length and weighing over 300,000 pounds apiece, with cabs to house the engineer and fireman. The B unit, sandwiched between them, had no cab and weighed eight tons less. Each unit was equipped with two V-type twelve-cylinder diesel engines. These turned the generators which supplied the power of two thousand horses to the eight steel driving wheels via traction motors. While one crew checked the mechanical systems from the engines which moved it to the brakes which stopped it, a second scrubbed away the grime from their stainless steel exteriors. Still a third crew fed its tanks with fuel and lubricating oil, water and sand. Both inspection and maintenance were meticulous; Number 437 would cruise at ninety-plus miles per hour. A mechanical failure at that speed could be disastrous.

In another part of the yard, the four sleeping cars, lounge car and glass-domed observation car were undergoing a different but no less thorough overhaul. Vacuum cleaners sucked the dirt of yesterday's journey from the carpets and upholstery, the linen and towels soiled by yesterday's passengers were replaced, the periodicals which carried yesterday's news removed. Telephones and radios were tested, toilets and washbasins disinfected, medicinal supplies and alcoholic beverages replenished according to a well-established formula: X number of travelers would demand Y number of aspirin and down Z number of cocktails. Door handles were polished and windows washed; complimentary items, ranging from stationery to sanitary napkins, were put in their proper places.

In still other areas of the mammoth yard sat the final components of what would shortly be train Number 437, Los Angeles to Chicago. Adjacent to the commissary department, the dining car was taking on the store of meat, produce and dairy products sufficient to supply six ample and varied meals, plus snacks. There would be no stop en route to restock the pantry; thanks to refrigeration, dehydration and freeze drying, none would be necessary. A mile away at the freight docks, the baggage car and the Railway Express car—identical in appearance save for the legends painted on their shiny skins—were being fed their cargo, precious and otherwise, from fork-lift trucks and belt conveyors and, on this particular evening, from an armored truck under the gaze of armed men.

Shortly after four A.M., a small diesel engine known as a switcher commenced to put the pieces together. Like an ant maneuvering prey many times its size, the switcher tugged first one section and then another from their various locations to the classification track where they were coupled together and finally to the outbound track from whence, a train at last, it would depart.

By six A.M., Number 437 stood beside the boarding platform, lacking only the crew which would pilot it and the passengers which would fill it, ready to be launched two hours later on its 2,200-mile journey. Thirty-six hours after that, it would pull into Chicago, barring acts of God . . . or schemes of men.

Willie Votaw, dividing his attention between the window beside his shoulder and the map on his lap, nudged the pilot. "We're coming up on it now. About a mile dead ahead." Yocum pushed down on the collective pitch stick, decreasing the helicopter's air speed and putting the craft into a gradual descent. Votaw unfastened his seat belt and scrambled down from the flight deck into the cargo compartment. The five men who sat or sprawled there regarded him expectantly.

"We're there," he announced. The others joined him at the open hatch, craning to examine the earth which lay a thousand feet beneath them. The terrain was mountainous, rounded foothills rather than lofty peaks, dotted with occasional broad valleys and laced by numerous small creeks. The hillsides were thickly covered with pine and blue spruce. Moisture from the previous evening's rain glistened in the morning sunlight, causing the forest to sparkle. In the grassy meadows and along the stream beds, their deciduous cousins—cottonwoods and ash and box elders—stood out in somber contrast, bare limbs providing splashes of gray and white to the predominantly green landscape. The wilderness, although a gentle one, stretched to the horizon in all directions, untouched and untainted, with no evidence to suggest that man had ever set foot there—save for the twin ribbons of steel which lay across it like some gigantic snake.

"That's the spot," Votaw said, pointing. "How do you like it?"

Bronko grunted. "Looks about the same as a dozen others to me. What's so special about it?"

"First, the meadow. We can land the Huey right alongside the tracks. Sure, it's not the only meadow on the line, but it is the only one that lies at the top of a three per cent grade. That, plus that switchback—over there, you can just see one end of it—means our train will be traveling at reduced speed."

"So what?" Hack wondered. "We're going to stop it,

anyway."

"The trick is to stop it exactly where we want to stop it, which is close to the chopper, right? You get rolling along with the throttle open—the sixth notch, say—and it'll take you at least a mile to stop, even with full service brakes. If our timing is off a few seconds, the train runs right past us."

"So it has to back up a few feet. Big deal."

Votaw gave him a sour look. "Nearest highway is eleven miles west. Nearest settlement is a ranch seven miles north. There are a couple of fire lookouts closer than that, but they're not manned during the winter. There's a radar station on top of that tallest peak over there, but they shouldn't spot us if we stay below their elevation. I tried to think of everything." He paused, inviting praise.

Heaston supplied it. "A damn fine job, Willie. Just one question. Since the line is single-tracked through here, is there any danger of another train plowing into ours while it's stopped?"

"Not with CTC. That's Centralized Traffic Control, the safety system all the roads use these days. There's this big electric board in the dispatcher's office, see, which shows the position of every train in his division. He controls all signals and switches from there, handles sidings and crossovers just by flipping a lever. The minute he sees our train has stopped, he'll give the red to any other trains, following or opposing, before they can enter our block."

"Hey, you mean they're going to know we stopped it—and where?" Hack asked, frowning. "I don't like that."

"Can't help it, pal. Everything's wired into the CTC board."

"That's why I've worked your tails off rehearsing this operation," Heaston reminded them. "Every extra second counts. We've got to be gone—and I mean long gone—

before they find out what's happened. Any more questions?"

"Wonder if there's any fish in that creek?" Moby Dick said, peering hopefully at the meadow.

Heaston grinned. "Maybe. If so, Guido can catch us a mess while he's waiting. He's got a whole day to kill."

"When I want fish, I get 'em from the butcher," Guido replied. "Say, why doesn't Dick take over for me? He could rig up a fishing pole and—"

"I want a trained operator on the radio to give us a fix. That's you, Guido. We'll be landing in the dark, you know, and we can't afford to set down in the wrong meadow."

In the distance, sunlight reflected from something that was not wet foliage but stainless steel. They watched with silent fascination the approach of a sleek train, its thunder lost in the clatter of the helicopter engine. It sped beneath them, unaware of their presence, and vanished with the track behind the nearby hills.

Heaston gave voice to their common thought. "Ours is coming, gentlemen. Let's go downstairs and get ready for it." He turned away from the hatch and took his previous seat on the box of carbines. The helicopter commenced a rapid descent.

Bronko sat down beside his colonel. "Only a few hours more. Don't reckon anybody can stop us now."

He looked at Heaston for confirmation. Since the others were looking also, Heaston put on a smile. "I'd say we're practically millionaires." There was no benefit to be gained by sharing with them the worry that nagged him, the question which throbbed in his mind with monotonous regularity. They could not answer it any more than he. The question was: Where's Duffy?

"We should be crossing the Colorado River any minute. Next stop—Williams, Arizona."

"One down, two to go," Clyde Munn said. "You were right about it not being California, Jake." He slouched in the roomette's only chair. Leslie was stretched out on the lower bunk and Duffy, when not pacing about the tiny compartment, perched on its edge.

"Why don't you try to get some rest?" she asked. "Nothing's going to happen for at least a few hours. Take the top bunk."

"In a little while. I've got a few things to check first."

"That's what you said when we left Barstow. Anyway, what can you check that you haven't already checked a half-dozen times before?"

Duffy had no answer; he could only give her a sheepish smile. In the sleeping car behind that in which they rode, the majority of his eighteen-man task force was in readiness. The remainder waited in the Railway Express car. Duffy was in touch with both detachments by walkie-talkie. The train crew was almost as readily accessible through the telephone in the corridor just outside the door. He was ready for battle; there was nothing he could do now except to wait for the battle to begin. Yet to justify his nervousness in the name of vigilance, he picked up the passenger list and began to study it.

"He'll have that darn thing memorized," Munn observed with a wink at Leslie. "If he doesn't have already. Give up, Jake. There aren't any of Heaston's people aboard. Not yet, anyway."

"Suppose you two get off my back for a while," Duffy said peevishly. "I've got to pass the time somehow."

"How about looking at the scenery? There's plenty of it out there." Munn gestured at the landscape gliding past the window. "Desert, mountains, forests . . . and it gets better as we go along. Relax and appreciate it, my boy. This may be your last opportunity."

"Now there's a comforting thought to relax with!"

"Didn't mean that quite the way it sounded. What I'm saying is that you're riding a train through the American West, probably the only unspoiled hunk of real estate left in this country. It can't last much longer and neither can the train as a people mover. So here's a unique opportunity to enjoy both before they disappear."

"One thing I've noticed about old cops," Duffy told Leslie. "They all turn into philosophers."

"Which is another way of saying bloody bores." Munn rose to his feet, stretching. "Okay, I got another suggestion. How about a spot of lunch?"

"You go ahead, Clyde. I'll be along shortly."

"I know. You've got a few things to check first. You, Doctor?"

"I don't usually eat lunch," Leslie told him. "If you wouldn't mind asking the steward to send me down a pot of tea, though—"

Munn promised to fetch it personally. After he had departed for the diner, she said, "Well, since you won't sleep and you won't eat, let's do the next best thing."

"Make love?"

"Hah! I doubt very much if you're up to that, either. I meant talk. Tell me what you're thinking, get it out into the open."

"There's the Colorado," he said absently. "Not much of a river here, is it? Looks shallow enough to wade across." He correctly interpreted her sigh to be reproach and turned to face her. "Bear with me, Leslie. I know I'm not very good company right now."

"For goodness' sake, Jake, you don't have to entertain me! I'm here to help, remember? And if I can act as a sounding board—"

He continued to gaze at her, but his eyes contemplated the imaginary rather than the real. "It's like a play," he said finally. "The script's already written. Heaston knows his part and I know mine, but neither of us knows the other's. We can only guess."

"But you have a pretty good idea what Heaston's part amounts to, don't you?"

"He's got to stop the train. He can't afford to wreck it because that might destroy the Bruegels and Loud wouldn't pay for that. So he's got to stop us some other way, maybe by creating a phony emergency, more likely by manipulating the signals."

"He might wait until the train stops itself, at a station, for instance."

"A station means people, telephones, the police close by. Heaston needs privacy and time, both to pull the hijack and get away afterward. No, he'll hit us somewhere out in the boondocks. This is how I see it, Leslie. Once we're stopped, he'll take over the engine to keep us stopped while he works on the Railway Express car. He blows off the door—they're all expert demolitions men—tosses in a tear gas grenade to take care of the guards—"

"Why tear gas? Why not a real grenade?"

"For the same reason he doesn't dare wreck the train. A fragmentation bomb might rip hell out of the paintings. Once the guards are neutralized, he loads the crates into the helicopter and he's off into the wild blue yonder. The whole operation shouldn't take over ten minutes, probably less. I'm sure he must have rehearsed it dozens of times with that old wood-burner back at Tres Muertos."

"Go on," she prompted when he appeared to have finished speaking. "That's only Heaston's part. What about yours?"

"I let him seize the engine because it doesn't really matter and I don't want the crew hurt. I let him blast open the Railway Express car and lob in his grenade. My men will be wearing gas masks. While he's going that, I send a small detachment to put the helicopter out of commission, cut off his retreat. The rest of us hit him from the rear and he's caught in the crossfire. Twenty of us against seven of them—it should be short and sweet."

"You seem to hold all the aces, Jake—surprise and superior numbers. So would you mind telling me what you're worried about?"

"Damned if I know," Duffy admitted. "Sure, I seem to hold all the aces. But I can't shake off the feeling that Heaston may be holding a wild card I haven't counted on."

Ralph Imel was looking for lost cows. The Rynerson Cattle Company ran over ten thousand head of prime beef on several times that number of acres of the unfenced rangeland which stretched from the railroad right of way on the east to the state highway on the west. During the winter months, the cattle were kept penned on the flatland, where they could be sheltered and fed. With the melting of the snow, they were turned loose to forage and fatten in the lush meadows. Imel's job was to guard them, brand them, eventually drive them to market . . . and, frequently, hunt for them. This made him a cowboy, the lineal descendant of the hard-bitten horsemen who had roamed the western plains a century earlier. However, Imel did not think of himself in such romantic terms; he preferred to call himself a ranch hand. All the same, his appearance fit the image of the pioneer cattle puncher. His lean body was garbed in well-worn levis, flannel shirt, and sheepskin jacket; a sweat-stained broad-brimmed hat shaded his leathery face. There were boots on his feet and gloves on his hands. He wore no pistol holstered at his belt—but then, neither had most of the earlier cowboys, legend notwithstanding.

Imel halted his horse on the crest of a hill overlooking the broad meadow which had no name but which was known to him and his co-workers as the Fying Pan because of its nearly circular shape and the gorge leading into it which could be the skillet's handle. He crooked one leg over the saddle horn and rolled a cigarette while he studied the flatland below. He was not surprised to find it empty. Cows, dumb critters though they were, seldom grazed that close to the tracks. The first train generally sent them stampeding down the canyons to break a leg or . . .

Imel paused in the act of moistening the paper as a movement below caught his eye. Something was down there, after all, not a cow but a man. He had been sitting with his back against the bole of a cottonwood tree near the creek; getting to his feet had revealed his presence. Who the hell? Imel wondered, and what the hell's he doing on our range? He fumbled in the saddlebag for his field glasses.

Their magnification did not answer either question. The intruder was a slender man with black curly hair whose natty jeans and whipcord jacket seemed more suited to a city park than a wilderness. Hunting or fishing, most likely, Imel decided. Since these activities as well as trespassing were prohibited on Rynerson Company land, he muttered, "Guess I'd better run him off 'fore he mistakes one of our heifers for a jackrabbit."

He kicked the mare's flank to move her forward and, in virtually the same instant, reined her in again. "Whoa, girl!" There was a box at the man's feet which Imel had assumed contained food and camping gear. It did not; from it, the stranger raised a tall skinny pole which was neither a rifle nor a fishing rod. Squatting, he placed earphones on his head and commenced to fiddle with what appeared to be dials.

"Rustlers!" Imel breathed. Rynerson, like the big cattle

outfits of the past, was plagued by raids on its herds. Today's cattle thief was considerably more sophisticated than his forebears, employing airplanes to locate and in some cases herd his prey and fast truck-and-trailer rigs to carry it off. And considerably bolder, since suspicion was not enough to convict and the punishment for rustling cows no longer came at the end of a rope. Imel had no doubt that the stranger was in the Frying Pan to scout the location of the herd and was reporting his findings by shortwave radio to his confederates elsewhere.

There were two courses of action open to him: Accost the rustler now or ride for reinforcements. Since the enemy was probably armed and he was not, Imel chose discretion over valor. He wheeled his horse about. With night coming, the dark-haired rustler wouldn't be leaving the Frying Pan immediately, certainly not on foot and with the bulky radio to carry. He might even be summoning the rest of his gang to join him there. Maybe if I hurry, Imel thought, we can grab the whole kit and caboodle of them.

One down and two to go, Munn had observed at lunchtime. Now, as they ate dinner, he reversed the equation. "Two down and one to go."

"Yeah," Duffy agreed, toying with the remains of his baked potato. Earlier they had safely passed the second of the possible danger zones. Shortly, they would be entering the third. Arizona and most of New Mexico lay behind the speeding train and, with them, the sun. They hurtled through a black countryside they could no longer see; the windows of the dining car gave back only their own reflections.

Leslie, who sat closest to it, could not refrain from attempting to pierce the darkness beyond. "Where are we exactly?"

"The last town was Springer. Next stop, Raton. After that"—he shrugged—"who knows?"

The waiter came by to suggest dessert. Leslie accepted; her two companions did not. Duffy also declined the offer of more coffee. "Might keep me awake," he explained gravely.

"I wish you hadn't told him that," Leslie chided. "He already knows we're sharing the same roomette even though we're not married. I don't mind—but darned if I want him to think you're bored with the arrangement."

Munn chuckled. "If you two are going to squabble, think I'll mosey along to the lounge for a cigar. Meet you on the platform, Jake."

"What'd he mean by that?" Leslie wondered.

"Raton's a division point. Clyde and I are going to walk around while the crews are changing, give the train the onceover, check Traffic Control just in case there's been anything peculiar reported up the line. I can't believe Heaston intends to wreck us, but there's no use taking chances."

Her sherbet arrived; Leslie took one bite and pushed it away. "I should have ordered something hot. Has it turned cold in here—or is it just me? Never mind, you don't have to answer that. I just realized for the first time what's actually going to happen." She gave him a weak smile. "Go on, say it. Just like a woman."

"I'm scared, too. Just like a man."

As they walked back to the sleeping car, they passed the conductor, who announced cheerily that the train would reach Raton in nine minutes. "Now I know how the Christians must have felt," Leslie muttered. "I'll bet there was some Jolly Joe like him at the Colosseum. 'Fasten your sandals, folks, nine minutes to the lions!' "

"There's one big difference. This time the lions lose."

Duffy hesitated at the roomette door. "Another big difference. The Christians didn't have a choice. You do."

"What are you suggesting, Jake?"

"There's nothing more you can do here except maybe get yourself hurt. We have a twenty-minute layover in Raton. Why don't you take a twenty-five minute walk?"

"It's the same old story. The woman's the last to be hired and the first to be fired. Sorry, you don't get rid of me that easily."

Cal Emery stood in the dispatcher's office, sipping a cup of coffee (Sanka, since caffeine acted as a mild diuretic and he would have no opportunity to relieve his bladder during the next two and a half hours) while he studied the big blackboard on the wall. Chalked there opposite the number of his train was the information he needed to know: the time it had arrived at the division point, the time it was scheduled to depart, the ETA at the next division point and the speed necessary to achieve it, other traffic in the same division. And, lastly, the names of the crew. Emery was pleased to see W. Jackson listed as the fireman. Bill had borrowed twenty bucks from him their last time out together. The way the line juggled assignments, an engineer might not ride with the same fireman more than a half dozen times per year. Tonight would give him a chance to collect his money before Bill forgot the debt or was transferred to another division.

Emery was a stocky gray-haired man of fifty-two whose conservative tie and dark business suit made him appear at this moment more an executive of the railroad than an operator of its trains. Only the gray-and-white-striped twill cap on his head gave a clue to his profession. The remainder of his working clothes, overalls similarly striped, were in the small satchel he carried. Following a custom long established (for what reason, no one could remember), he would not don them until he entered the cab.

Emery drained the mug. "Have this washed and ready for me when I get back. Might try washing the pot, too."

The dispatcher reacted with mock indignation. "It was washed—just before Christmas." He shoved a clipboard at Emery. "Sign here. Your usual X will do."

"Any last-minute S.O.'s, Manny?"

The dispatcher riffled through the stack of teletype flimsies, looking for changes or corrections which might not have been transferred to the blackboard. "Nope. You're clear to roll."

"How about that rough spot south of the K12 siding? I got a lot of vibration there last time out."

"Track gang cleaned it up yesterday. New ties, new ballast. You can highball all the way."

Reassured, Emery signed the register, acknowledging that he had received and understood all instructions and was, therefore, solely responsible for carrying them out. The conductor was the captain of the train, but the engineer was its pilot and on his shoulders rested its safety. His final act was to compare his watch with the standard clock; the smaller time piece synchronized exactly with the larger.

"Your crackerbox is right on the dot so far," the dispatcher called after him. "Try to keep her that way, okay?"

Emery strode down the platform past the cars which waited on the ready track to the three-unit engine at their head. His fireman—a title which wasn't accurate these days, since the diesel-electrics had no fires to tend—was already there, making his pre-departure exterior inspection. Emery was surprised to discover that he was a stranger. "Where's Bill?"

"Didn't they clue you? Jackson took ill all of a sudden. They tapped me to fill in for him." The fireman extended a greasy hand. "Charlie Victor."

Emery scrutinized the stranger, a gaunt man a few years his junior. "New around here, aren't you, Victor?"

"Just transferred in from the Newton division." Victor grinned. "But I've been down the line enough times to know the way."

The boast, though probably justified, did little to relieve Emery's annoyance. Never mind that he could not now collect the debt owed to him. Why did the office have to assign him a fireman he didn't know and without even telling him about it?

Victor had begun the check of the fuel, water and sand supplies; they completed it together. As he put on his overalls, Emery conceded grudgingly that the man seemed to know his stuff. Oh, well, no use making a federal case of it; it wasn't his railroad. He slipped into the padded seat on the right-hand side of the cab and adjusted it to the height he found comfortable, giving him a clear view of the tracks twelve feet below. Victor took his place on the opposite side of the cab. "Two minutes," he announced.

While waiting, Emery manipulated the switches above his right shoulder which operated the headlight and the windshield wipers; they functioned properly. At the one-minute signal he started the diesel engines and placed a hand on the throttle at his left and the other on the brake lever at his right.

The signal lights changed from red to green. "Green board," Emery said. "Horn."

"Green board," Victor repeated and pulled on the cord which dangled from the cab's ceiling. The air horn emitted a warning blast. Emery released the brakes. Simultaneously, he pulled the throttle lever back into the first notch, exciting the generators to turn the twelve driving wheels barely enough to stretch the draw bars between the cars. He watched the ammeter needle. When it reached 200, he pulled the throttle into the second notch, tightening the draw bars and draft gears the length of the train. The ammeter needle continued to climb, but the train remained as motionless as before. At the third throttle notch, the hum of the engines became plainly audible. With a barely perceptible jerk, the train commenced to creep forward. It serpentined slowly from the ready track to the outbound track, steel wheels clattering through the crossover, and left the yards at five miles per hour. Emery divided his attention between the ammeter and speedometer, moving the throttle from one notch to the next in response to the dancing needles. At the eighth—and final—notch, he allowed it to remain until proper cruising speed was reached, then eased it back to the sixth notch. Full power was not necessary to keep the train at constant pace on level track; momentum was also a factor.

"Running test," he told Victor. He cut the power, allowing the train to coast on momentum alone. He applied the air brakes lightly then, satisfied that they were in working order, released them and restored power. "Guess we're in business. Nothing for us to do now except sit here and mind the store for the next couple of hours. Something bothering you, Victor?"

"Just a helluva cold, that's all," his fireman replied, reaching for a handkerchief. "Can't seem to get rid of it."

Anthony Heaston lay face down in the grama grass alongside the embankment as the train roared past. The ground shook from its passage as from a bombardment. As both noise and vibration faded, Heaston got to his feet, stamping about and beating his hands together to drive away the cold. Along the empty track, the others did the same. The relief was only ephemeral. In these foothills of the Rockies, the thermometer plummeted with the disappearance of the sun; it stood now at near freezing. A light fog mantled the meadow and more issued from their mouths with every exhaled breath. Yet the chill they felt was not wholly physical.

It's always the same, Heaston reflected; whether it was your first skirmish or your hundredth, the fear invariably was there. Neither training nor experience quite eliminated it. A man might control his muscles, keep his hands from shaking and his bowels from loosening, but not even the most stolid could control his imagination. In these final moments before battle every soldier was a coward. What was counted bravery was merely how successfully you mastered your cowardice. Each found his own amulet to rub, tangible as a rabbit's foot or intangible as prayer, to ward off the horror which began with the unspoken words, *What if I* . . .

Heaston, who did not believe in God or trust in luck, had learned to assuage his fear by assuaging the fear of others. He walked slowly down the roadbed, stepping from tie to tie, pausing to offer a word of reassurance or ask a question of the black-garbed men who waited there. Their replies ranged from Bronko's terse grunt to Moby Dick's nervous giggle. Hack Plum mouthed profanity softly like an incantation. Guido was performing a little jig while tossing the tear gas cannister from one gloved hand to the other.

His final stop was at the helicopter. The Huey squatted fifty yards west of the track, its undercarriage hidden in the ground fog which made it resemble a ship adrift on an ocean of mist. Yocum stood in the cargo hatch, clutching his amulet, a bottle of whiskey.

"Better go easy on that," Heaston cautioned. "You're the only one who can pilot this magic carpet."

"I fly better drunk than sober. Drinking beats thinking, anyway." He hesitated. "I was wondering, Skipper—Bronko ever say anything to you?"

"About what?"

"Oh, nothing. Now's no time to talk, anyway." He put the bottle to his lips.

Something was bothering Yocum; Heaston decided it was the same malady that infected all of them and, thus, not worth delving into. "Start your engine as soon as the train stops," reminded. "Liftoff should be four minutes, thirty seconds later."

He rejoined the others. Bronko was squatting beside the track, one hand resting lightly on the nearest rail as if he expected to feel the vibration of the train they could neither see nor hear. "What's keeping her?" he grumbled.

Heaston consulted his wrist watch. "The flyer passed by here right on schedule. The next one should be our gravy train. Another five minutes."

"Suppose Willie wasn't able to pull it off?"

"Then we'll light the flares." Heaston squeezed his shoulder soothingly. "Let the dust settle, Bronko. We'll know which way to jump when she hits the switchback. If Willie doesn't sound the horn . . ."

Bronko knew the battle plans, primary and contingent; nevertheless, he could not refrain from questioning them. "What if the flares don't stop her, either? Maybe we should have figured on wrecking her." Heaston made no reply nor did Bronko expect one. The die was cast and it was too late now for maybes.

The edge of an orange saucer showed itself above the jagged horizon, rising slowly. There was silence save for the rasp of their breath and the song of the crickets along the creek. From the hills above them came a sudden startling howl, a coyote baying at the moon; far off, like an echo, another added his voice to the mournful refrain. "Damn varmints," Bronko muttered. "Like to take me a rifle and—"

"Listen!"

From the distant blackness came another sound which was produced by no throat, animal or human. It was the faint rumble of steel wheels on steel rails.

Leslie said, "I miss the old-time train whistle. There was something so romantic about it. A horn doesn't even begin to compare. Why is it blowing now, anyway?"

"We're approaching a grade crossing."

"How can you be sure?" Not that she really cared, but keeping the conversation going helped relieve her jitters. Leslie had given up directing her questions at Duffy, however. His body perched on the bunk beside her but his mind was elsewhere. Since entering the final climactic lap of their journey, he scarcely seemed aware of the other two persons who shared the roomette.

"Two long, one short, one long." Munn, with less at stake, was willing to chat. "Every toot has a meaning all its own. Two long blasts, proceeding normally. Three short ones, stop at the next station. And so on. If you ever hear six short blasts, brace yourself for a mighty sudden stop—"

As if that had been a cue, Duffy leaped to his feet. "We're slowing down!" His ears, tuned to the train rather than the conversation, had detected a change in the rhythm of wheels on rails unnoticed by the others. An instant later the decrease in speed became apparent to them also. "There's no stop scheduled here. This is it!" As Munn lunged for the telephone in the corridor, he seized the walkie-talkie. "Duffy to task force. Red alert! Red alert!"

"Hold it!" Munn leaned around the jamb, the telephone to his ear. "It may be a false alarm. The engineer says we're being shunted onto a siding to let oncoming traffic pass."

"Like hell! There's no other scheduled train on this line. Heaston's jimmied the signals. Stay on the phone, Clyde; have the engineer keep you posted on what he sees." As the train continued to slow, he ordered Leslie to turn off the roomette's lights and to lie on the floor.

"Engineer says we're just entering the siding," Munn relayed tensely. "No sign of trouble so far."

Duffy knelt by the window and raised the shade a few inches, peering into the night. The radiance of the rising moon was sufficient to cast the shadow of the train upon the ground; it inched forward like a gigantic caterpillar. There was a slight jolt as both train and shadow came to a halt. Nothing moved on the gravel-covered embankment, in the grassy ditch or among the trees beyond. "Come on, come on," he softly begged the enemy he knew must be there. "What are you waiting for?"

"You're right about there being no other scheduled train in this block," Munn reported. "The one we're waiting for is a special. Ordinarily, we'd be the superior train and they'd have to go into the hole for us. Don't know yet why this one's different."

"There isn't any special train, that's why."

"Something's coming just the same. See for yourself."

Duffy scrambled over Leslie's prostrate figure to the corridor. A quarter mile to the north, the weaving beam of a headlight signaled the approach of another train. The beam grew rapidly larger and more distinct until he could distinguish the blunt nose of the engine and the white running lights and white flags which designated it as a special. Suddenly, it was upon them with an avalanche of noise and a rush of air which caused their own train to quiver. Then it was gone, leaving behind only the swiftly fading click-clack of its wheels. Almost immediately the streamliner commenced to move out of the siding in the opposite direction.

"I don't get it." Everything pointed to this being the attack—and yet the attack had not come. Of course, Heaston didn't know about the special train any more than we did, he thought, attempting to rationalize away his chagrin; he wasn't expecting us to be sidetracked here. Heaston was still waiting for them somewhere down the line. That had to be the answer. He informed his task force of his conclusions via the walkie-talkie.

Leslie asked plaintively, "Is it all right if I get up now?" He turned on the roomette's lights and assisted her to rise. "That was the longest five minutes I ever spent."

"I wish I could tell you that you're not going to have to go through it again. Consider that a dress rehearsal."

Munn slumped onto the bunk beside them, another victim of letdown. He said wearily, "That wasn't just any old special. It was a very, very special. President Carson's funeral train."

"I thought they held the funeral a couple of days ago."

"Services in Washington yesterday. Burial tomorrow at Alamogordo, O.K.'s home town. I understand the President's flying out, him and all the high-mucky-mucks. The body went by train because Mrs. Carson's got a thing against airplanes."

"Oh," Duffy said, and there was silence.

"It's really ironic," Leslie mused. "The timing of it, I mean. That O.K.'s funeral train should be traveling the same track on the same night that his old enemy, Colonel Heaston—"

Duffy leaped to his feet with a yell that was nearly a scream. "Oh, my God!" He seized Leslie by both shoulders and shook her. "What was that you told me last night—

that Carson had planned his funeral years in advance, down to the last detail? You don't mean he did it personally, do you?" He didn't wait for her startled lips to form an answer. "Of course, he didn't! Hell, no, that's not the way generals operate. They give the orders and some flunky draws up the details—some lousy colonel in the Pentagon basement that the Army didn't have any other use for. I should have guessed! His wife practically told me, raving about how they rubbed his nose in . . . and that explains why it had to be Heaston for this job. Nobody else would do because nobody else knew the plans."

"What are you talking about?" Leslie gasped. "Jake, stop shaking me!"

He didn't appear to hear her. "I had everything figured out," he groaned. "All of it—except the most important thing. Heaston isn't after the Bruegels; he never was. He intends to steal O.K. Carson's body!"

Cal Emery chuckled to himself as they hurtled by the sidetracked streamliner. Not often that you got the opportunity to make a superior train go in the hole and especialy the L.A.-Chicago hotshot which stopped for no one. He imagined that his brother engineer was burning at the delay which would put him into La Junta at least five minutes behind schedule. Sorry about that, buddy, Emery thought, and didn't mean a word of it. Since one or the other must have tardiness chalked against his record, he preferred it be the other guy.

Emery's own record would show that his train was precisely on time. Once past the switchback they were just entering—the Fishhook they called it because of its configuration—they'd be at the crest of the grade. He could let out the throttle for the remainder of the relatively straight and level journey. In one hour and thirteen minutes,

Number 319 Special would roll into Raton on the black, i.e., as scheduled. Then it would be up to his relief to keep it that way.

This evening Emery felt a mild regret at the regulation which confined his tenure to one division, a space which allowed for a maximum of two and a half hours' throttle time at normal speeds. Crew fatigue was the cause cited by the unions, although the companies charged featherbedding instead (and Emery secretly agreed). Whichever, he would have enjoyed piloting this particular train all the way to its destination. Wasn't often that a man was given this kind of an assignment, carrying the body of his former commander-in-chief to its final resting place. Emery, like millions of his countrymen, had served under Orrin Kell Carson in war and voted for him in peace and felt honored to have done both.

Emery regretted also, though more deeply, that he would not be able to bid a personal farewell to the soldier-President. But the casket rested in the flag-draped baggage car directly behind the three diesel-electric engines under military guard. Neither could he hope to pay his respects to the living. The President's widow, their son and his wife rode in the private drawing car, outfitted like an apartment, in which Carson had campaigned and later, the presidency behind him, traveled extensively about the country in deference to his wife's abhorrence of flying. Behind that, a similar car held the remainder of the funeral party, longtime friends and more distant relatives, Edith Carson's personal physician and the Army honor guard which consisted of an officer, eight enlisted pallbearers, a bugler, three flag bearers and four riflemen. Even if security had permitted him to intrude, decorum did not. Emery felt sure that his passengers had retired early in preparation for the grueling day ahead.

At least I'll be able to say I had a hand in it, he thought; it would be something to tell the grandkids. He stared ahead at the twin ribbons of steel rushing toward him twelve feet below, noting the familiar landmarks revealed by the headlight as it described its figure-eight pattern. They were nearly at the crest of the grade.

A blast of the horn made him jump. "What the hell!" he ejaculated while his hands flew automatically to throttle and brake levers.

"Sorry," his fireman apologized. "Lost my balance and grabbed for the first thing I could lay my hands on." Sheepishly, he indicated the air horn cord.

"You scared the bejeezus out of me," Emery reprimanded. "Don't never do that again, Victor. Suppose you'd made me take my foot off the dead man's control?" The fail-safe device on the cab floor was designed to halt the train in case the engineer suffered a heart seizure or other disabling accident. Should his foot leave the pedal for longer than two seconds, engine power was automatically cut off and full service brakes applied. The emergency measure was only slightly less damaging than the crash it was intended to prevent. Sudden braking—"dumping it" in railroad parlance—would cause the wheels to lock, the train to skid and, even at a speed no greater than fifteen miles per hour, the passengers to tumble about like rag dolls. Emery, a thirty-year veteran, was well aware of all this. While nothing so trivial as a squawk from the horn could spook him into activating the dead man's control, it did no harm to remind Victor of the possibility.

Furthermore, the incident served to justify his previous indignation at being assigned a strange fireman. Now he'd really have something to throw in the dispatcher's teeth. *You know what that dumb bakehead went and did? Pulled the calf's tail, thinking it was* . . . Then compassion intervened. Victor wasn't a bad sort. No use giving him a black mark over something that didn't amount to a hill of beans, actually.

They reached the crest of the grade, a spot Emery could sense rather than see. Ahead stood the signal lights which marked the beginning of a new block. Beyond them lay a broad valley that resembled a black lake in the moonlight.

"We're on the downhill leg now," he told his fireman happily. "Green board." He waited for Victor to repeat and thus affirm his reading.

Victor did not. "Red board!" he said loudly.

Emery was startled for the second time within minutes. He squinted at the signal lights in case he was mistaken. He was not; all three vertical lights glowed green. "You color blind or something? That board's as green as grass."

"I say it's red—and it's what I say that counts."

Emery discovered to his utter consternation that Victor held a pistol and that its muzzle was pointed at his head. "For God's sake, man! What do you think you're doing?"

"Stopping the train. Better hit the wind." As Emery continued to gape, he warned, "If you don't brake her, I'll put a bullet in you and let the dead man's control do the job. You can save a lot of broken necks by cooperating—including yours."

Death stared from his face as well as the pistol muzzle. Emery reached for throttle and brake levers. Number 319 Special, bereft of power and robbed of momentum, commenced to slow.

The conductor, jiggling the toggle key of the shortwave radio, repeated "437 to Raton CTC. Come in, please. Roger, Raton. Stand by." He removed the headset and passed it to Clyde Munn who, in turn, thrust it at Duffy. The conductor did not leave his stool, however; the presence of the other two men in the tiny radio cubicle made movement impossible.

Leaning over him, Duffy put the earphones on his head and the microphone to his lips. "This is Inspector Duffy, FBI. I must get an urgent message to the special train that passed us a few minutes ago heading south. The one that's carrying President Carson's body. Can you contact them?"

"Hold on a minute," the traffic controller replied. That minute passed and then another before he spoke again. "Can't seem to raise 319. They must have had an equipment failure."

"Keep trying. This is an emergency."

"Still no answer," the controller reported. "Now that's peculiar," he continued in a startled tone. "My board shows that 319 has stopped in Block 17. Can't figure out why; there's been no stop ordered. Say, is that the emergency you mean?"

"That's it," Duffy agreed with a groan. The funeral train's unauthorized halt and its radio silence could mean but one thing: The hijacking of O.K. Carson's body was underway. He gripped the conductor's shoulder. "How far past Block 17 are we?"

"This is Block 16 we're in. Five, six miles maybe."

"I want this train stopped immediately. Maybe if we back up we'll still be able to get there in time."

"Don't tell me," the conductor said, shaking his head to indicate that such matters were out of his hands. "Tell CTC."

Duffy got virtually the same response from the traffic controller, perhaps even (though he could not see it) the same shake of the head. "I don't have that kind of authority." Who did? Only the division traffic manager, who unfortunately could not be reached immediately. Nor would the controller take the responsibility on his own shoulders.

"I got trains coming in both north and south," he explained. "I let you go into reverse and it screws up my whole board. No telling what might happen. Suppose 319 decides to back up too? It's possible—and with her radio out, you could plow right into her."

With every second carrying him farther away from the battlefield, Duffy gave up the argument. "Okay, okay—but will you at least stop this train long enough for me to get off? If I can't get back to Block 17 any other way, I'll walk!"

The controller had a better suggestion. "I've got a southbound freight on J42 siding, waiting for you to pass. You should reach her in about three minutes. If it'd be any help, I can redlight you there and you can grab a ride back to 17 with her."

"Do that." He dropped the headset in the conductor's lap and thrust Munn out of the cubicle. "Help me get my people rounded up. We're changing trains in three minutes."

"What good's that going to do?" Munn asked, following him down the swaying corridor. "By the time we get there, the whole thing'll be over. Probably over already, for that matter."

"Probably," Duffy agreed without breaking stride. "But I can't go by probablies. There's just the slimmest chance that Heaston ran into delays he wasn't expecting. Or that his helicopter won't start."

"Or that he got struck by lightning. I'll lay you a hundred to one that Heaston's pulled it off without a hitch, slick as a fox stealing chickens. Better face up to it, Jake. You're licked."

Duffy could not refute the dour prediction; both logic and intuition argued to its correctness. Yet he refused to accept the corollary, that the contest was over. Heaston, the wily fox, might have succeeded in raiding the coop and carrying off his prize. It remained for Duffy, the tenacious bloodhound, to track him to his lair.

Anthony Heaston opened the steel door and motioned the others to enter. The four men maneuvered their burden through the narrow opening and over the high sill and set it down gingerly.

The room could have been better described as a compartment, resembling the wardroom of a warship. The bare floor and low ceiling were gray steel plates, the rivets plainly showing. The walls were fashioned of the same metal but had been painted in pastel tones of blue and green. There were no windows. Air flowed into the compartment by means of wall ducts. Illumination was provided by fluorescent tubes in the ceiling whose sterile light dispelled shadows. Inset in one wall and stretching from floor to ceiling were two identical electronic consoles, their faces boasting a bewildering assortment of meters and dials and gauges, while their keyboards were studded with an equal number of knobs and switches. In the opposite wall was a second oval opening, a doorway without a door. This gave access to an even smaller compartment outfitted with two pull-down bunk beds, a toilet and a washbasin. The beds were the only items of furniture in either room—unless you cared to count the swingaway stools attached to the consoles.

In this bizarre setting, the presence of the five men who still wore the black nylon coveralls and black stocking caps donned for their mission did not seem incongruous—nor did the flag-swathed casket around which they stood silently. They might have been creatures from an alien planet celebrating some exotic form of worship.

Hack Plum shattered both the silence and the illusion. "Let's open 'er up," he suggested. "I'd like to take a look at the old fart."

"Knock that off," Heaston told him sharply. "O.K. Carson was a good soldier and a great general. We'll give his body the respect it's entitled to."

"I just wanted to make sure he's really in there. Be a shame if they'd slipped us a ringer."

"They didn't. They couldn't have known about us. So keep your hands off. That goes for everybody." Heaston softened his tone. "I haven't had a chance to tell you before, so I will now. You really had your stuff together. Well done, gentlemen."

"You gonna give us medals, Skipper?" Guido asked with a grin. "I'd like one with a blue ribbon, to match my eyes."

"Afraid I can't oblige—but how does a million bucks strike you as a substitute?"

"Well, there's one thing you can say for money. It goes with everything. How long to payday?"

"Just as soon as the government can get it together and we can count it."

"Hope they don't drag their feet," Votaw muttered. "Things could get mighty smelly around here."

"That shouldn't bother you, Willie. That cold of yours might turn out to be a blessing in disguise, ever think of that?"

Moby Dick squeezed his immense bulk through the oval doorway. He blinked his colorless eyes painfully against the fluorescent light. They located Heaston. "Aircraft's refueled and lashed down, Colonel."

"Where's Ace?"

"He said to tell you he'll stay with the chopper."

"Which means Ace is tending to a little refueling of his own," Guido interpreted.

"No doubt," Heaston agreed. "He's been hitting that bottle hard recently. Anybody know what's bothering him—aside from the obvious?"

Bronko and Hack exchanged glances and Bronko said evenly, "I wouldn't worry about it. Ace always did booze it up pretty good."

"I suppose." Heaston clapped his hands briskly. "Our job isn't over yet. Hack, you and Willie take the first trick on guard. One inside, one outside—settle that between yourselves. The rest of you turn in. I'll sit up with the General for a while."

"There's only two bunks for three men," Guido pointed out. He winked at the others. "One fair way to settle it. I'm thinking of a number between one and ten. Guy who guesses closest to it sleeps on the floor. You first, Dick."

The albino giant screwed up his face in painful concentration. "Seven," he said finally.

"How about that? Seven's the very number I was thinking of. No use the rest of us guessing now. The floor's all yours, Dick."

"I don't get it," Moby Dick grumbled as he followed Guido into the sleeping quarters. "Don't make no difference what number I pick, I lose every time."

"The law of averages," Guido enlightened him.

Heaston sat down on one of the swingaway stools. "Better grab that other bunk before Dick figures out he's been had," he advised Bronko.

"He never will. Some folks are born losers. Anyway, I feel more like gloating than sleeping. Ten—million—bucks. Try saying that real slow and then tell me if that ain't the sweetest music this side of heaven."

"I know an even better tune. I—did—it." Heaston indicated the casket with his toe. "The most audacious guerrilla raid in history, Bronko. And I pulled it off without firing a shot or losing a man. No matter what happens from here on in, they'll never be able to take that away from me."

Bronko regarded him with a mixture of admiration and wonder. "You're a strange bird, Colonel. I never have understood what makes you tick. Doubt if there's a man alive who does."

"Oh, there may be one." Heaston chuckled. "I'd sure like to be able to see Jake Duffy's face right this minute."

FOUR

> Hub said, "Don't quit now, we're in it still,
> Once past the grade and it's all downhill.
> A little more speed and, once again,
>   Winner's gonna be The Gravy Train."
>
> Fireman screamed, "We're goin' in the ditch!"
> But Hub replied, "You son of a bitch,
> Keep bendin' your back and don't complain,
>   Just trust in me and The Gravy Train!"
>
> They were nearly home, just one mile more!
> When her boiler blew with a mighty roar,
> Shook the clouds till they started to rain
>   On what was left of The Gravy Train.
>
>   —The Ballad of The Gravy Train

Number 319 Special could no longer accurately be called a train, since the three-unit engine had been detached, merely a cut of cars. The cut sat amid others in a remote corner of the marshaling yards in Albuquerque out of sight of the terminal and out of reach of the news media. The communiqué supplied them said tersely that the train had been delayed due to Edith Carson's sudden illness; she was undergoing treatment by her physician. Requests to interview the doctor or other members of the official party were denied. Did this mean the former President's burial would be postponed? The spokesman declined to speculate.

Duffy's credentials enabled him to get as far as the track on which 319 stood. A cordon of armed soldiers, the honor guard reinforced by a contingent of military police from the nearby airbase, barred him from reaching the train itself. Their orders were to allow no one to approach within one hundred yards and to shoot anyone who attempted it. The stringent security measures were less to prevent outsiders from entering the train than to prevent the truth from leaving it. For the moment, the government was treating the theft of O.K. Carson's corpse as top secret information. Even the train crew was being held incommunicado.

Duffy was able to command use of a telephone in the stationmaster's private office. From the upper-floor window he could see 319 while he attempted to direct the hunt for the precious cargo it had contained. The reports he received were uniformly negative. Neither the North American Air Defense Command in Colorado Springs nor the FAA radar net had recorded tracking the helicopter which had carried off the casket. No airfield within the craft's cruising range had refueled it. His task force of special agents was scouring portions of five states for other possible landing sites, since the helicopter could not remain aloft indefinitely. With first light, the search on the ground would be abetted by a search from the sky. Duffy succeeded in getting commitments from the Civil Air Patrol, the U.S. Forestry Service and the Air National Guard in both Colorado and New Mexico. The Air Force required authorization from higher headquarters, but he felt confident that it would be forthcoming.

He was still at the telephone when, an hour before dawn, two black limousines preceded by a police sedan entered the yards. The procession did not halt at the terminal but made its circuitous way through the maze of tracks to the funeral train. The cordon of soldiers parted to allow the vehicles to pass. The limousines disgorged their passengers beside the private drawing car. Two men went quickly up the steps; the remainder formed a second cordon around it. The President of the United States had arrived accompanied as always by the Secret Service.

Duffy could guess the purpose of the emergency meeting. The President had been summoned hastily from Alamogordo for a personal briefing and, more importantly, to settle the question: What do we do now? Duffy could conceive of only one possible answer. Nevertheless, those in the drawing car appeared to have some difficulty in arriving at it. The sun was lightening the eastern horizon before the President and his aides hurried down the steps. The three-car procession commenced to retrace its route. It halted briefly near the terminal to disgorge a passenger, the President's companion. Duffy saw that it was F.X. Raymond.

Raymond was surrounded by newsmen when Duffy reached him. His normally ruddy face was nearly as white as his bushy hair and he was replying to the questions with a monotonous "No comment." He took Duffy's arm gratefully. "Thought you'd be around someplace. Come on, Upp wants to see you."

"I've been trying to get in for hours," Duffy explained as they crossed the tracks. "The guard stopped me. They wouldn't even relay a message."

"You're lucky. If Upp had known you were here, he might have ordered you shot. God, what a mess!"

"Would it help to say I'm sorry?"

"I'd advise you to say as little as possible. Let me do the talking."

Upp was awaiting them in the comfortably appointed

parlor of the drawing car. His eyes had the haggard look of one who had suffered a public humiliation as well as a personal loss, but his bearing was as rigidly correct as ever. There was a second man present; Duffy was introduced to Arthur Carson. The son was a younger copy of his famous father, with much of his charm but little of his fire. He alone of the four was able to muster a smile.

"This is the man I was talking about," Upp informed him. "The young mastermind who was guarding the wrong train in the wrong place going in the wrong direction."

Duffy, remembering his instructions, said nothing. Raymond spoke for the defense. "Let's be fair, sir. Jake was nearly correct in his deductions. If it hadn't been for the unfortunate coincidence of the Bruegel shipment—"

"Oh, a spendid job! Of course, he let the criminals pull it off and get clean away—but what does that matter since his theory was correct? He did manage to capture a bunch of cowboys, though. Or was it the other way around?" He cut off Raymond with an impatient gesture. "Let him speak for himself, F.X. As I recall, Mr. Duffy is an eloquent young man."

"I don't know who captured who," Duffy said sheepishly "I guess you could call it a standoff." The freight had returned him and his task force to the meadow too late to intercept Anthony Heaston, too late even to board the funeral train which had departed—but in time to run head on into the Rynerson Company posse. "They thought we were cattle rustlers. We thought they were Heaston's men. There were a few shots fired before we got things straightened out. Luckily, nobody was hurt."

Upp snorted. "Can't even shoot straight! But I agree it was lucky in this instance."

"If I can offer something in my own defense . . . At least, I was able to provide instant identification of the hijackers and—"

"Don't take any bows for that. Heaston identified himself. Made no bones about it. Stepped in here bold as brass, stood right where you're standing now and presented his demands."

"May I ask what those demands are, sir?"

"Ten million dollars cash. To be delivered by midnight, approximately eighteen hours from now." Upp gritted his teeth. "He explained that he didn't want to rush us, since he realized it might be difficult to round up that amount of currency in a hurry."

"Delivered where and how?"

"It's to be left in a baggage car on a siding near where the hijack took place," Raymond explained. "Unmarked bills, of course. Twenty-four hours after Heaston collects the ransom, he'll notify us where we can find General Carson's body. That's to give him time to get out of the country, undoubtedly."

"Eighteen hours," Duffy said thoughtfully. "Not much time, but it should be enough. Especially since we're not starting from scratch." He swiftly related the steps he had taken to locate the gang's hideout. "They obviously haven't left the area. Where the ransom's to be delivered proves that they've holed up close by. I can mount a search that'll cover every square inch of territory, by plane, by car, even on foot if necessary. I already have the Air National Guard and the CAP and I expect to have the Air Force. With them to cover the air and my own men, plus the local police, to cover the ground, we'll collar Heaston before sunset for sure."

"There'll be no search," Upp said flatly. "I thought you'd been told. We intend to pay the ransom."

"You can't be serious!" But a glance at their expressions told him they were. "For God's sake, why?"

"I should have thought that would be obvious, even to you. This isn't a simple game of cops-and-robbers, Duffy. The only thing that matters here is that we recover General Carson's body."

"Certainly, sir, and the best way to do it is to catch Heaston."

"I don't agree with you and neither does the President. We feel that the matter can be handled more expeditiously and discreetly our way."

"Discreetly," Duffy repeated. "Now I'm beginning to understand. You mean to cover this up, don't you? I completely forgot that this is an election year."

Raymond uttered what sounded like a groan, but Upp surprisingly did not take offense. In a patient almost kindly tone, he said, "Try to understand what's involved. Orrin Kell Carson was a former President, a war hero and an international figure. He was the most beloved man of his time. At this very moment he's being mourned not only here at home but all around the globe. Can you imagine what the effect will be if we announce that his body has been stolen while on the way to its final resting place? It goes farther than domestic politics. This nation will appear foolish to our friends and weak to our enemies."

"If we submit to extortion, that's exactly what we are. The truth's bound to leak out, anyway. Too many people already know about it."

"They'll keep their mouths shut. The interment will take place at Alamogordo as scheduled—with an empty coffin, of course. Once we've recovered General Carson's body, we'll be able to deny any stories as wild fabrications."

"While the gang gets away clean with ten million bucks. And don't tell me that you'll deal with Heaston in due time. He can't be arrested or prosecuted or punished unless he's charged first. And you can't charge him without revealing the truth—which you don't intend to do."

"That may be true. I say we'll just have to make the best of it."

"And I say that makes you Heaston's accomplice. You're giving him ten million dollars that don't belong to you. That money belongs to the taxpayers."

"Are you suggesting we hold a national referendum?" Upp retorted. "I've already explained why we must pay the ransom. You may challenge the decision but I believe even your precious taxpayers would agree that the President is slightly more qualified to make it than you are."

"Presidents aren't always right." Duffy swung toward Arthur Carson. "I mean no disrespect, sir, but that includes your father. I'm thinking of the Do Binh affair. He tried to sweep it under the rug, and what happened tonight is the direct result. If Anthony Heaston had been given justice fifteen years ago—whether he was convicted or exonerated—we wouldn't be fighting him now. Can't anybody see that we're making the same mistake again?"

Arthur Carson pursed his lips. "I do know that Dad always regretted the way he handled the Heaston case," he admitted. "And I'm not sure that if he were here today—" However, he lacked the strength to renounce a decision in which he had already concurred. "But since the President and his advisers have made their decision, I don't feel it's my place—and because of Mother I wouldn't want to do anything that . . ."

"Exactly," Upp concluded. "The ransom is being collected. The burial will proceed as planned. The search will be discontinued immediately. I don't ask your approval, Duffy. I do demand your compliance."

"I'll go you one better. I'm submitting my resignation. I won't be a party to this."

"Your resignation is accepted," Upp snapped. "However, I would remind you—in case you have some notion of telling the story to the world—that your oath binds you to silence, whether in government service or not. The penalty for divulging top secret information—"

"I know the law," Duffy retorted with equal heat. "What I didn't know was that it doesn't apply to everyone. Thank you for enlightening me." He spun on his heel and stalked out of the parlor. As he went down the steps, the drawing car rocked, but not because he had slammed the door; the engines were being coupled to the train to convey it on the last lap of the journey.

Raymond caught up with him as he crossed the tracks to the terminal. "Don't say it," Duffy advised him. "I'm sorry if I embarrassed you, F.X., but that's all I'm sorry for. I'm right about this and you know it."

"Maybe you are and maybe you aren't. All I wanted to say is don't be in too much of a hurry to put your resignation in writing. I happen to know that Upp plans on stepping down soon. Once he's out of the way, I'll see that you're reinstated. Till then, cool it, okay?"

"No sale, F.X. I'm going after Heaston."

"You can't do that, Jake! You don't have any authority. You resigned your badge."

"That's right." Duffy smiled mirthlessly. "But I didn't resign my citizenship."

Leslie left the train at La Junta with the intention of returning to Los Angeles by air, where the Bruegel paintings, no longer in jeopardy but still her responsibility, waited in a bank vault. At the last moment, impelled by what she termed curiosity but what was actually a stronger emotion, she switched to an Albuquerque flight. She sat now in a hotel room near the airport and watched the object of her curiosity (or whatever) pace back and forth.

"I estimate you've done at least a mile already," she observed. "I'm pooped just watching you."

"What? Oh—sorry. I think better on my feet. If it bothers you—"

"It doesn't. But I can't see it's helping you, either. You can't fight the entire world. When you've done everything possible, it's no disgrace to lose."

"It's no great honor, either."

"Jake, when are you going to admit the truth? You've turned what should have been a job into a holy crusade, a duel to the death between you and Colonel Heaston. Can't you see how foolish that is?"

"Go ahead and say it. No man is infallible. You can't win 'em all. Et cetera, et cetera."

"I'll say it because it's true." She adopted a soothing tone. "If you won't quit, at least have the sense to get a little sleep. You're practically out on your feet."

"Yeah, okay." But he turned instead to the dresser and began again to study the map spread out there. "Three thousand square miles," he muttered. "If I only had a clue where to start—"

Leslie snatched the map away. "In your present condition, you couldn't find Heaston if he were in the next room. You're going to take a rest, and don't you dare argue with me!"

He managed a reluctant grin. "You sound just like a wife."

"You know," she agreed with a note of surprise, "I do believe you're right. Well, be that as it may . . ." She pointed imperiously at the bed. "Lie down and go to sleep. Immediately!"

He obeyed the first command but could not obey the second. He stared at the ceiling while she removed his shoes and covered him with a blanket. "God, to come so close!" he grumbled. "To have it figured down to the last detail, everything except . . . But how could I have imagined that Heaston was planning something so unique as stealing a dead President?"

"You couldn't. It isn't actually unique, though. It happened once before, nearly a hundred years ago. A gang tried to steal President Lincoln's body back in 1876. Except that they were caught before they could pull it off."

"Really? I didn't know that."

"Well, I wouldn't have known it myself if I hadn't read it recently. There was this article in one of those historical journals Ira Niblo keeps in his waiting room. As a matter of fact, Niblo wrote it himself."

Duffy sat up as if he had received a jolt of electricity. "Good God—of course! How could I be so stupid? Not only the wrong crime but the wrong criminal!"

"I don't understand."

"I tabbed Julian Loud as Mr. Zeus, the brains behind Heaston. As long as the Bruegels were the target that made sense. But what would Loud want with Carson's body? He may be peculiar, but I can't believe he's collecting corpses of famous men—and he certainly doesn't need the ransom money. But I'll bet a certain overworked and underpaid Lincoln scholar could use a couple million right nicely. And since Niblo was borrowing the boss's ranch, what was to stop him from borrowing the boss's alias? Quick—what time is it in California?"

"A few minutes after seven, I guess," Leslie replied, bewildered by the apparent incongruity of the question.

Duffy fumbled in his hip pocket with one hand while reaching for the telephone with the other. "Switchboard, I want to place a station-to-station call to Los Angeles." He located the folded slip of paper in his wallet. "Area code 213. Number is 663-9543."

"Jake, what on earth! Who are you calling?"

"A friend. At least, I hope she thinks so after I wake her up."

As he expected, Pamela Frain was still in bed. Her sleepy voice quickened with pleasure when she learned the identity of her caller. "Jake darling! What a lovely surprise! Where are you, anyhow?"

"With a lady doctor in Albuquerque, New Mexico."

Pamela giggled. "Quit your kidding."

"Pam, are you still playing private secretary to Ira Niblo?" She was; Niblo's regular girl had suffered a relapse, necessitating her return to the hospital, and consequently Pamela . . . Duffy cut off the explanation. "Where's Niblo now?"

"Well, he's not here, if that's what you're insinuating. I like my job, but not that much." For that matter, Niblo wasn't even in Los Angeles. He had left the previous day for a vacation in Aspen, Colorado. Pamela found the picture amusing. "Can you believe Mr. Niblo on skis?"

"There's almost nothing about Mr. Niblo I wouldn't believe. Thanks a million, Pam. Thanks ten million, in fact."

"Hey, not so fast! What about dinner tonight?"

"My advice is to accept the first offer you get." He hung up and grinned delightedly at Leslie, more refreshed by what he had learned than by a dozen hours of sleep. "Grab your coat, sweetheart—and make it a warm one. We're off to Mount Olympus. If Zeus can't tell me where Heaston and his myrmidons are hiding, nobody can."

He was not the only one to have gone without sleep that night or to pace a hotel room that morning. But while Duffy had spent the hours hopscotching across the map by train, plane and automobile, Ira Niblo's traveling, though equally fatiguing, had been entirely mental.

Anticipation had kept him glued to the radio throughout the night, waiting with tingling stomach for the bulletin that would herald success of the coup. Apprehension continued to hold him there long after the rising sun summoned his fellow vacationers from the lodge to the snow-covered slopes. Their exhilarated shouts and the clatter of the ski lift came faintly to his ears, but Niblo was not aware of them. He prowled the cheery room like a prisoner on Death Row, conscious of nothing but the radio which might reprieve him from the dread that grew larger with each passing moment.

Though he switched feverishly from one station to another, the reprieve did not come. Edith Carson's illness, which had caused the funeral train to be delayed for a few hours in Albuquerque, had been diagnosed as emotional fatigue. The interment of Orrin Kell Carson would proceed as planned although delayed somewhat, with full coverage via radio and television. Listeners and viewers were urged to stay tuned.

To Niblo, aware of the presidential visit to the funeral train but not of the presidential decision arrived at during the visit, the news indicated only that the little army had not been able to halt the train or, more likely, had been routed in the attempt. Whichever, the result was the same: disaster.

He wondered now how he could have ever been so foolish to embark on such a doomed enterprise. Months ago, when he and Bronko Shaman first conceived the plan, it had seemed the answer to his prayer. Years of embezzling Julian Loud's money (telling himself he was merely borrowing it while knowing he was not) had finally caught up with him; Loud was beginning to suspect the truth. Niblo knew that he could no more hope for mercy than he could hope to replace the stolen million from his inadequate salary. His first timid foray—skimming the casino receipts from the Xanadu with Bronko's connivance—had failed ignominiously. And then Bronko had chanced to mention Anthony Heaston, the disgraced soldier who had been the one, by an incredible stroke of fortune, to draw up the plans for O.K. Carson's funeral. *Steal O.K.'s body? You're out of your mind, Niblo! Am I? It almost happened once before—with Lincoln—and if we knew in advance the route the train would take and were able to recruit the right men . . .* Painstakingly, he had worked it out, from the prison break in Colombia to the hijack in Colorado, embezzling even more of Julian Loud's money in the process against the day when the ransom would enable him to replace it all—with enough left over to permit him to live comfortably ever after, free of peonage. Oh, it had been brilliant, all right . . . and yet, somehow, it had failed, as everything had always failed for Ira Niblo.

He was caught between the consequences of his embezzlement and the consequences of his crime, with no way out. Save one. His suitcase contained a loaded revolver. Niblo hefted the weapon in his hand for perhaps the dozenth time that morning. He had stood on the brink of suicide before and always drawn back, unable to shed that last faint hope of salvation. He could not shed it now. Heaston and his men might be dead or captured, but there was no reason to assume that he must share their fate, whether prison or death. His part in the hijacking was obviously still unknown. Otherwise, the police would already have come to fetch him. It might yet be possible to evade both the law and Julian Loud.

A knock on the door made him jump. "Who is it?" he asked tensely.

"FBI—open up!" The words rang in Niblo's ears like

the trumpet of doom. His eyes roved wildly from door to window and back again, seeking escape and finding none.

"Open the door, Niblo!"

"Just a minute," he quavered. With a shaking hand, he placed the pistol against his temple.

The door was flung violently open. Niblo knew the mustached young man who plunged across the threshold, but his dazed mind could not recall his name.

"Put down the gun, Niblo! You don't want to kill yourself." The imperious almost scornful tone, so reminiscent of another's, struck him like a slap in the face, paralyzing his will. The young man held out his hand. "Give it to me."

Niblo surrendered the revolver with an odd sense of relief as if, in ridding himself of the weapon, he was also ridding himself of responsibility. He no longer feared punishment; all he desired now was absolution. *Shrive me, Father, for I have sinned* . . . "I didn't want to do anything wrong, you have to believe that, I didn't have a choice." In his urgency to be understood, he was not aware that he babbling any more than he was conscious of the tears streaming down his cheeks. "Mr. Loud, he'd have crucified me, don't you see? I didn't have anywhere to turn, there was no one who cared, no one at all, everyone was hounding me—"

"Sit down," his confessor suggested gently. "And tell me all about it."

In the fading twilight, the prairie resembled a dark green sea. The evening breeze caused the buffalo grass to ripple like waves which rolled majestically toward the gray-black mountains. Here and there the bare branches of an oak tree broke the undulating surface, flotsam adrift on an ocean of vegetation. But on this ocean as on others more authentic, there was no sign of life save for the craft apparently anchored there and the tiny crew it contained.

"I still can't see anything," Leslie said, squinting through the car's windshield. "Nothing but acres and acres of weeds."

"That's the whole idea. This place was designed to present a zero-degree profile."

The apparently empty plain was a former intercontinental ballistic missile base, one of nearly a score the Air Force had constructed in the early 1960's to house the Titan and Atlas rockets on which the American nuclear deterrent then depended. Each base was composed of six separate and self-contained sites, widely dispersed for insurance against attack. Each site, in turn, housed three missiles in concrete silos 160 feet below the surface, shielded from above by massive doors of steel and concrete three feet thick. In their nests, the deadly birds stood poised on elevators, ready for the signal which would send them on a flight across the top of the world. Smaller silos contained the radar antenna and the personnel elevator. A network of subterranean tunnels connected silo to silo and to a number of other rooms as well—propellant mixing plant, equipment storehouse and the igloo-shaped control center in which the monsters' human servants ate and slept and kept their vigil with terror. The air-conditioned city beneath the earth, built and equipped at a cost of over one billion dollars, had long since been abandoned, phased out by the advent of the more reliable solid fuel Minuteman. Titan and Atlas had departed, not on towering pillars of flame, but meekly on trucks which conveyed them to the scrap-heap. Their base, impossible to move, remained for some future generation to marvel at, a monument both to man's ingenuity and his folly, like the pyramids of the pharaohs.

"According to Niblo, Heaston and Company are holed

up in Charlie Site. If I read these blueprints right, that would put them over there, about a mile northwest of us." He added, "And about fifty feet down, of course."

"Where do you suppose they hid the helicopter?"

"In one of the missile silos. They're forty feet in diameter and the elevators are designed to hold over one hundred tons. Lower the copter into the hole, close the doors and nobody would ever suspect it's there."

"It's certainly a perfect hiding place," Leslie admitted. "Imagine them ever finding it!"

"Well, it wasn't exactly luck, you know." Julian Loud had sold the land to the government originally, his Ruidoso Construction Company had been the prime contractor and, when the base was declared surplus, his Forte Enterprises had repurchased it for a fraction of the original cost. Loud would, no doubt, sell the land again someday at an even higher price; to turn not one but three profits from a single property was typical of him. Ira Niblo had attempted to turn a fourth, his own. Months earlier, he had caused Charlie Site to be refurbished and its air, water and power systems put in working order (with utmost secrecy, since that was the way Julian Loud did everything) on the pretext that microfilm records of the Loud financial empire would be stored there. At the moment, however, Charlie Site concealed only a helicopter and eight men, one of them a corpse.

"You said that Julian Loud was putting up the money for the hijacking," Leslie mused. "And you were right. He just never knew about it."

"If it's irony you want, consider Niblo. He believed he'd lost when he'd really won. He was so sure the holdup had failed that he was ready to blow his brains out. He doesn't know even yet how close he came to collecting. Maybe he never will." Ira Niblo—or the shattered creature which bore that name—lay sedated in the detention ward of a Denver hospital, still repeating an incoherent confession to which no one listened. "Sanitarium or prison cell, that's his future."

"And the others?" She indicated the seemingly lifeless prairie. "What about them, Jake?"

"Their future depends on how good a poker player I am. My future too, I guess." The last rays of the sun still tinged the white cumulus clouds with pink, but night had come to the land beneath. The distant mountains were rapidly fading silhouettes. "It should be dark enough in another twenty minutes."

"How soon do you expect the rest of your men to get here?" When he did not reply or look at her, Leslie seized his arm. "Jake, surely you're not thinking of going in alone!"

"I thought you understood that," he replied impatiently. "I've got to talk to Heaston."

"They'll kill you!"

"I don't think so. Either they'll buy my proposition or they won't. If they do, fine. If they don't, well, maybe I can keep them arguing about it until reinforcements arrive."

"Then I'm going with you," she declared.

"No, you're not. You're going to drive like hell for the closest phone. The President and his party are spending the night at the Air Force Academy in Colorado Springs. You can reach Raymond there. If he moves fast, he should have his men here in less than an hour."

"Then why not wait? Phone Raymond yourself and ask him to send help instead of rushing in alone."

"Because I'm pretty sure there wouldn't be any help forthcoming. I've got to force the government's hand, leave them no alternative."

"That isn't really the reason," Leslie said slowly. "That's

simply an excuse. It's that damn hubris—the only way you can satisfy it is to beat Heaston man-to-man. For God's sake, be sensible! Is pride worth dying for?"

"I don't know. But it's the only thing I've ever found worth living for."

"You—man!" She spit it out like a curse. "I thought you were different, but you're as stupid as the rest, playing your idiotic games and telling yourself they're really important to anyone. There's a lot of things worth living for, and pride is only one of them. There's love and doing good and making other people happy . . . but go on! Commit suicide or blow up the world—what does it matter if it satisfies your previous vanity?" She ran out of breath and finished in a whisper, "You're no better than the men you're chasing, Heaston and the others. They call him Mad Anthony, but you're as crazy as he is!"

"You may be right," he admitted with a sigh. "But—Mad Jacob? It doesn't have the right ring somehow. Dumb Duffy is more like it."

As the night swallowed up the automobile and the sound of the engine which powered it, he reflected that Leslie, in her anger, had hit the nail squarely on the head. An idiotic game she had called it. It was—like war or football or bullfighting, and women were right to scorn them. Yet their more practical natures failed to take into account (and perhaps this was the real difference between the sexes) the male's deep-seated need to test himself against nature, against other males and, above all, against the image he held of himself. To meet the challenge was all that mattered, win or lose; to shirk it was unforgivable. Duffy, who saw his own image clearer than most, could acknowledge the idiocy of the game. At the same time he could not abandon it without abandoning everything that made him what he was.

He began to walk, setting his course by the evening star, toward the destination he knew was there but could not see. The wind was chill, yet the earth beneath his feet was still warm with the heat of the day. He moved slowly to avoid stumbling into holes concealed by the tall weeds, but not stealthily. Heaston must certainly have posted a guard as any good military commander would; Duffy did not wish to take them unawares.

He passed one of the three ICBM silos, its concrete collar capped by the massive doors. His recollection of the blueprints told him that he was within a hundred yards of the entrance to the missile complex. He cupped his hands to his mouth and shouted, "Ahoy, Charlie Site! I want to talk to you. I'm coming in alone."

There was no reply. Duffy continued his slow advance, hands held high in the air, pausing twice to repeat his call. He felt certain that he had been both seen and heard, but no challenge came from the darkness. Ten yards from the entrance shaft he halted. "Ahoy, Charlie—"

A hard pointed object jabbed his spine. A voice advised, "Pipe down. Charlie hears you," and Duffy was relieved to learn that the sentry was Guido Faccialorda rather than the trigger-happy Hack Plum. The former guerrilla had allowed him to pass his place of concealment in order to take him from the rear. "Hands behind your neck. Reach for a gun and you're dead."

"I'm not armed." Guido frisked him expertly for weapons just the same. "I came to parley, not fight."

Guido attempted a feeble bluff. "I don't know what you're talking about. This is private property, mister. There's a law against trespassing."

"There's also a law against robbing trains. Cut the con, Guido. I didn't buy it back on the Tres Muertos and I don't buy it now."

His captor chuckled. "Thought I recognized you. How's the movie business, Duffy?"

"Like yours—in the hole. Can we go below now? This night air's hell on the sinuses."

"Well now, that's a shame. We're not running a home for stray cops, you know."

"I can pay my way. Take me to Heaston and I'll prove it."

Guido signified agreement with a jab of the carbine. At the entrance to the silo he commanded Duffy to spread-eagle himself face down on the dirt while he spoke into the intercom. Shortly Duffy felt the earth beneath him began to quiver and he heard the whir of the elevator as it ascended to the surface.

"All aboard," Guido said, nudging his captive with his foot. He followed Duffy into the empty elevator. The door closed behind them; the steel mesh cage commenced a slow descent. A second sentry awaited them at the bottom of the shaft. On the prairie above, the night was chill; here in this realm of perpetual artificial daylight, the air was hot and humid. Moby Dick had stripped to the waist, causing his pallid hulk to resemble a miniature iceberg. His colorless eyes regarded Duffy curiously, neither friendly nor hostile. He turned and led the way down the sloping tunnel, which was wide enough to admit an automobile. Guido brought up the rear, whistling softly and tunelessly through his teeth.

The single-file procession passed through pools of light cast by bulbs recessed in the ceiling, turned into an intersecting tunnel equipped with a heavy blast door which stood open. Beyond this lay a smaller door, oval-shaped like an aircraft hatch. The second door was also open. Duffy stepped from the dimness of the tunnel into the brilliance of the control room with the outward nonchalance but inner trepidation of an actor entering a stage.

His audience awaited him expectantly. Because of the paucity of furniture, only two of the men were seated. The other three squatted on the gray metal floor or leaned against the pastel walls. Their sober expressions and the presence of the flag-draped casket in the center of the room made the gathering resemble a wake.

Anthony Heaston rose to his feet with a smile. He alone appeared unconcerned at Duffy's presence; in an odd fashion, it seemed to amuse him. "Welcome to Charlie Site," he said pleasantly. "I believe you've already met everyone, that is, with the exception of—"

"I've met him, too. How's the cold, Willie?"

Votaw took a step forward to peer at him. "The guy from the plane!"

Hack said angrily, "Then we've got you to thank for this, huh?"

"All I got from Willie was the overlay to your map. The one who told me where to find you was Ira Niblo. Or Mr. Zeus, if you prefer."

Heaston retained his calm. "I thought so—since Niblo was the only other person who had that information. I'll admit I'm not entirely surprised you're here. I've had a gut feeling about you all along."

If Heaston was not surprised, Duffy was. From their first meeting, he had sensed this duel between the two of them must lead inevitably to some such final confrontation. He had not expected that Heaston would sense it also. "Funny how life works out," he said slowly. "I wouldn't be here now if O.K. hadn't had the same kind of gut feeling about you. He's the one who put me on your trail in the first place."

"I've wondered about that. So it was the General, was

it? He had a fantastic intuition at times—frightening almost. Yours must not be too bad, either, Mr. Duffy. How far behind us were you last night?"

"Not far. I just happened to be riding the wrong train."

Heaston laughed with genuine amusement. "That's marvelous! Well, you seem to have made a fast recovery. Bronko, give Mr. Duffy your seat. He must be fagged out after all the chasing around he's done. Sorry I can't offer you a meal this time, but we're on short rations, as you can imagine."

"I didn't come to eat. I came to pick up a package." Duffy indicated the casket.

It was Bronko's turn to laugh, but the sound held more contempt than merriment. "You ready to cough up the ten million?"

"I'm ready to offer you something much more valuable—your lives." He paused to allow that to sink in. "Gentlemen, you've played a good game but you've lost. We arrested Niblo this afternoon and he spilled his guts. We know it all, the hideout down in Mexico, the bank accounts Niblo set up abroad where you planned to stash the money—we even have the phony passports he got for you. Of course, I hardly need to mention that Charlie Site is completely surrounded by federal agents."

"My God!" Votaw whispered. His consternation was mirrored in varying degrees on the countenances of the others. Only Heaston appeared unmoved; he continued to regard Duffy intently. Of his men, Bronko was the first to recover. "Hack, you and Guido get topside for a recon, find out what we're up against. Tell the fuzz we've got Duffy and if they want him back alive—"

"Hold on," Heaston interrupted. "Let's analyze the situation a bit before we go off half-cocked. Like, for instance, why Mr. Duffy came down here alone instead of at the head of his army. I believe we don't have to look any farther for the answer than the coffin there."

There was a moment of silence and then Guido breathed "Yeah!" and Bronko said, "I read you, Colonel. Nothing's really changed, has it? We've still got our ace in the hole."

"Exactly. The government may want us—but not nearly as bad as they want General Carson's body, safe and sound." Heaston swiveled his stool to face Duffy. "Here are our terms. You call off your men and pay the ransom, every last dollar of it. Otherwise, we destroy the body."

"Would you actually do that?" Duffy asked curiously.

"You bet your life we would!" Bronko snapped. "Hack, where'd we stow the plastic?"

"Storeroom." Hack scrambled to his feet. "Want me to fetch it, Bronko?"

"Take a look at this first," Duffy suggested. He reached into his coat and brought forth a folded copy of the *Denver Post*. He held it up for all to see. "Read it and weep, gentlemen. General Carson was officially laid to rest at one o'clock this afternoon in Alamogordo, New Mexico—and here are the pictures to prove it."

Bronko snatched the newspaper from his hands. His incredulous gaze darted from the headlines to the casket over which he stood. "It's some kind of trick," he muttered. "It's got to be."

"We've been had!" Hack raved. "I wanted to open the damn thing, remember? I told you so! The coffin's empty!" He began to tug frantically on the flag which covered it. Guido seized his arm, but Hack threw him off, cursing.

"That coffin isn't empty," Duffy said loudly. "The one in Alamogordo is, though." Having recaptured their attention, he went on in a lower tone, "The point is that nobody knows that except you and me and a few others. As far as the rest of the world is concerned, General Carson is safely tucked away in his marble tomb. They saw it happen on television, right before their eyes. That makes the actual body superfluous. It no longer has any real value. Oh, we'd like it back if possible—but we're certainly not going to pay ten million dollars for it."

"He's bluffing," Guido declared, but his tone carried no conviction and none of his companions lent support, either by voice or expression, to his verdict. The newspaper passed silently from hand to hand and finally was tossed crumpled into a corner of the control room.

At last Heaston chuckled. "It appears that our ace in the hole has turned into the joker. Well, Mr. Duffy, I believe you came here with a proposition. I suggest you make it."

"In exchange for General Carson's body, I'll give you two hours' head start. That should be enough for you to reach Mexico. Once you're out of the country, you're safe. We won't follow you past the border."

Heaston raised his eyebrows. "I'm surprised. I didn't expect you to be quite so generous."

"I'd rather see you all behind bars," Duffy admitted frankly. "But I don't think I could put you there without a fight. Nobody's been killed so far, and I'd like to keep it that way."

"Then we're to understand that you're offering us amnesty?"

"Not exactly, but that's what it amounts to. You haven't committed a capital offense, not yet. Stealing a body is only grand larceny, not kidnapping. If you fly quietly away—and never come back—there'll be no charges filed. If you don't, we'll have to blast you out, and O.K. Carson won't be the only dead man in this king-size gopher hole."

The threat stirred the others, but whether to defiance or toward submission he could not tell. He kept his eyes on their leader, for whom the proposal was primarily tailored.

Anthony Heaston was not one to surrender meekly even in the face of certain death. Neither, Duffy felt certain, was the ransom of paramount importance to him; he had played the game for the joy of winning it rather than for any financial reward. Thus, the proposal which would allow him to emerge with at least a standoff and with his forces unscathed, the concern of all good commanders. On the other hand, there was also the strong possibility that Heaston—like Custer, to whom he had sometimes been compared—might choose glorious extinction to honorable retreat. Duffy waited tensely to learn if he had judged his foe correctly.

He had; Heaston said slowly, "I accept your proposition." He gazed around at his Hellions with a sigh. "The ending isn't exactly what we hoped for—but we did accomplish what we set out to do, didn't we? At least, we won a moral victory. We'll have to be satisfied with that."

"To hell with your moral victories," Bronko said in a gutteral voice. "Maybe that's enough for you, but it sure ain't enough for me. I went into this for the dough and I mean to get it. So, okay, the government won't buy Carson's body. There's somebody somewhere who will, maybe his family. I hear they got plenty socked away. We'll put it up for bids, see what—"

Heaston sprang to his feet. "When did you start giving the orders, Bronko?"

"You dumb farmer," Bronko replied contemptuously, "I've been giving them all along. I always did, even back in the old days. Go ahead and ask them who really ran the outfit. Ask them who wet-nursed them and gave them their passes and saved their skins and saw they had food to eat and booze to drink and money to spend. Me, that's who! And who the hell planned this caper and set it up and made it run? You'd still be rotting down in Colombia if it wasn't for me."

Heaston's expression was a mixture of incredulity and anger. "So it's mutiny, is it?"

"Wake up and smell the coffee, Heaston. You're not in the Army any more. They kicked you out, remember?" Bronko whirled to face the others. "Can you believe it? He's telling us to throw in our hands again just like he did back in Nam. Anyone here forget what happened to us then? Trust me, he said, I'll see that you get justice. Well, we got the stockade and we got busted and we got bad conduct discharges! But that's nothing to what we'll get this time if he has his way."

"Listen to me, men! What he calls my way is the only way you're going to get out of here alive. Follow him and you're dead. Is that the kind of a leader you want?" Heaston gazed expectantly from face to face. "Make your choice—Bronko or me."

Moby Dick said promptly, "I'm with you, Colonel, all the way." None of the other men spoke; one or two looked away. Heaston paled perceptibly, but he managed to keep his voice crisply confident. "What about you, Willie?" Votaw shrugged and kept his gaze fixed on the floor. "Guido?"

"You've got to understand our position, Colonel," Guido said uncomfortably. "Auld lang syne and all that crap is great as far as it goes—and I got nothing against you personally. But Bronko—"

"Ace?"

Yocum hesitated, an indication that he was not wholly committed to the rebels, and Duffy thought that Heaston had made a tactical error in not seeking his support first. The pilot was the most valuable ally of all, since only he could fly the helicopter. Bronko realized it, too. "I'll speak for Ace. He votes for me. Right, Ace? You're not forgetting

Mindy, are you?"

Heaston blinked. "What about Mindy?"

"Never mind. Ace understands."

Yocum licked his lips. "Sorry, Skipper. I don't have any choice."

"Same goes for Hack, though I guess he'd be stringing with ol' Bronko, regardless." His mouth split in a grin. "Looks like you've done been relieved of command, Colonel. No hard feelings, though. You can still come along for the ride if you like. You too, Dick."

"I stay here," Heaston told him quietly, and the giant albino, bewildered but still loyal, moved to separate himself from the rebels and to stand beside his commander.

"Losers belong together," Bronko said with a shrug. "Ace, get the bird warmed up. Guido, you and Willie and me'll tote the coffin. Hack, you stay here and make sure these three don't cause us any trouble. I'll buzz you soon as we're ready to fly."

"Why bother?" Hack wondered, picking up his burp gun. "Let me chop 'em now and we won't have to worry."

"Negative. Duffy's right about one thing. We haven't done anything yet they're likely to extradite us for, nothing they can prove, anyway. But if we go around killing people we don't have to, especially an FBI man, why, they'd never stop chasing us. No chopping, Hack, and that's an order." He tempered mercy with a threat. "As long as they behave like good little boys, I mean."

"They'll behave, all right." Hack motioned with the burp gun toward the sleeping quarters. "In there. First man to stick his head out gets it blown off."

Bronko gave Heaston a mocking salute. "I hope they give you better quarters at Leavenworth than they did down in Colombia. Only don't go looking for me to spring you this time."

Heaston did not reply. He strode stiffly into the makeshift cell. Duffy and Moby Dick followed him.

Anthony Heaston slumped on the edge of the lower bunk, hands clasped between his knees and head bowed as if in prayer, the picture of dejection. The repudiation by his Hellions, those men closest to him in all the world and his substitute family, had apparently shattered him as nothing else had succeeded in doing. Moby Dick hovered anxiously over his idol, wishing to console him but unable to find the means.

Duffy sat against the opposite wall, only slightly less dejected. He had based his strategy on the assumption that the swashbuckling colonel was the dominant figure among the outlaws. The tardy realization that Heaston was merely a paper tiger struck him as a crushing blow. He had known that in their duel there could only be one winner; it had never occurred to him that there might be two losers.

Heaston's shoulders commenced to shake and Duffy thought he was crying. An instant later, he realized the other man was laughing. "Heaston's Hellions," he chortled. "And all the time it was really Bronko's Bastards!"

"Aw," Moby Dick said comfortingly, "don't you go believing that, Colonel. Bronko never was worth two hoots in hell."

Heaston patted the huge white belly affectionately. "Good old Dick, loyal to the end. But you're wrong about Bronko. He's a tough soldier with plenty of grit, a first-class fighting man. His mistake is in assuming that's enough to qualify him for command."

"He seems to be doing all right so far," Duffy observed.

"Bronko has one fatal flaw. He always underestimates the enemy. He's demonstrated that here. He's decided because he was able to outmaneuver me that I'm all washed up. Hack's a stupid animal, but his instincts were better than Bronko's in this case. He should have let him shoot me."

"He may yet."

"A prime rule for guerrillas operating in enemy territory is: Don't take prisoners. You'll only regret it later. It's up to us to make Bronko pay for violating that rule." He raised a questioning eyebrow. "Or am I taking too much for granted by including you, Mr. Duffy?"

"That depends on what you mean to do, Colonel."

"I stole General Carson's body once. I intend to steal it again."

"Then count me in. I never expected you and I would be fighting on the same side, but since we are, you'd better call me Jake."

"Good," Heaston said briskly. "Our first chore is to get out of here. What's Hack's position?"

Duffy glanced through the oval doorway at their guard. "Still sitting on the other side of the room, him and his itchy trigger finger."

"We gonna make a break for it?" Moby Dick asked in a husky whisper.

"No. Only one man at a time could get through the door, and Hack would pick us off like ducks on a pond. I'm sure he's hoping we'll try." Heaston got to his feet and sauntered across the cubicle toward the lavatory.

"What're you doing?" Hack challenged.

"No harm in a man relieving himself, is there?" He accepted Hack's grunt for permission, used the toilet and flushed it. The angle hid him from their guard's view and the rushing water concealed the sound made as he lifted the porcelain lid from the tank. Duffy wondered if he intended to use the lid as a weapon or a shield; it seemed a poor choice for either. However, Heaston set the lid aside and unscrewed the round brass float which activated the tank's cutoff valve. Holding it concealed, he returned to the bunk.

He did not retake his seat. Instead, he turned back the mattress to reveal a latticework of flexible steel bands, each secured to the frame by small springs. He removed one of the bands and passed it to Moby Dick. "See if you can bend that in two without breaking it." The albino's huge hands performed the task easily, manipulating the metal as though it were putty. Heaston asked softly, "What color are your shoelaces, Jake?"

Duffy had to look before he answered. "Brown."

"I'll take one if you can manage to give it to me without Hack seeing."

Duffy rose, conscious that the muzzle of the burp gun rose with him. "Stretching my legs," he told its owner. He did not dare join his fellow prisoners, since that would put all three men out of Hack's sight and might cause him to become suspicious. He approached the doorway instead. "Happen to know what time it is?"

"Why?" Hack asked sarcastically. "Got a heavy date?"

"Just wondering. My watch stopped."

"Get back where you was and stop asking damfool questions."

Duffy shrugged and returned leisurely to his former position. He no longer wore two shoelaces but one; Heaston, lying on his stomach, had taken advantage of the concealment provided by the high threshold to remove the other. He used the cord to fasten the U-shaped steel slat to the bronze float. Duffy saw why he had required his shoelace rather than his own. Its color nearly matched the dull bronze of the float as Heaston's black lace would never have done. However, he could still not imagine what function the finished product was intended to serve.

Heaston held it up for their inspection. "What does that look like at first glance?"

It was, surprising, Moby Dick who supplied the right answer. "Maybe—a grenade?"

"Good boy. And what does a soldier do when he sees a grenade come flying in? Hits the deck, of course."

"Maybe," Duffy said dubiously. "And maybe he won't buy a toilet float and a bed slat for a grenade."

"Just a matter of conditioning. Be ready to move and move fast." Heaston went to the doorway, holding the crude replica hidden at his side. "Hack, can I talk to you for a minute?"

"Forget it, Colonel. Me 'n' you got nothing to talk about."

"I wanted to ask if you remembered a chap back in Nam—Benny Moreau, used to be called Big Mo. Buddy of yours, wasn't he?"

"Reckon he was. So what?"

"Happen to recall what became of him?"

"Don't see how I could help it," Hack replied, drawn into the conversation against his will. "Being as I was right alongside when that VC grenade blew his head off. I must have puked for a week afterward."

"I thought you'd remember," Heaston murmured. He lobbed the dummy grenade at Hack's feet and plunged into the control room with Moby Dick and Duffy close on his heels.

If they were quick, their jailer was quicker. Instinct had sent Hack diving to the floor to evade the anticipated blast. A second instinct brought him to his knees to fend off his enemies, the burp gun pointed at their leader.

The hammering explosions reverberated from the steel walls like thunder. Yet it was not Heaston who received their deadly charge. In the last instant, Moby Dick flung him aside. The point-blank volley, sufficient to tear an ordinary chest to bits, staggered the albino giant but did not stop him. His huge hands closed about Hack's throat. Falling, his immense body crushed him to the floor.

Duffy snatched up the burp gun. The weapon was no longer needed. The two former comrades were linked in death as they had been linked in life; like the gingham dog and the calico cat, they had destroyed each other. Heaston attempted to pry them apart, but he could not. Moby Dick's hands clung to Hack's mangled throat with a grip impossible to dislodge.

"You goddam fool," Heaston said softly, the curse like a benediction, and Duffy saw that there were tears in his eyes. Yet he was too much the soldier to indulge in sentimentality. "What the hell are you standing there for? Get topside! Call in your men to stop the Huey before it gets away!"

"There's just one problem, Colonel. I don't have any men to call in. I came after you alone."

Heaston stared at him incredulously. "Alone?" He began to laugh. "My God, Jake—what a team you and I would have made! We could have beaten the devil himself."

"We can get around to the devil later." Duffy motioned toward the tunnel. "Right now, let's start with his disciples."

Heaston studied the control consoles. "They've opened the silo doors," he muttered, interpreting the lights which glowed on the twin boards. "But they haven't raised the elevator yet. They're warming up the chopper first. Soon as it's ready, they'll be calling for Hack."

Static crackled from the intercom to validate his prediction. Bronko's voice rasped, "Hack, we're set to go. Lock your prisoners in the control room—secure both doors—

and get down here on the double."

"Roger," Heaston growled in a fair imitation of the dead man's voice. "You heard the orders, Jake. On the double."

"Why can't we close the silo doors and trap them?"

"There's a second control panel in the silo itself that can be used independently of these to operate the doors and the lift. So they could raise and lower the rocket to tinker with it without taking the risk of firing the damn thing, I guess. We held a couple of dry runs this afternoon. At the time I thought it was a pretty dandy system. Now I'd like to murder the guy who dreamed it up."

"What you're saying is that we've got to capture the helicopter."

"Capture it or cripple it, whichever plays the best. Once she's airborne, we've had it. Come on." Duffy matched his stride down the sloping tunnel. "What's that coffin made of?" Heaston mused. He answered his own question. "Phospher bronze. Who should know that better than the guy who drew up the specifications? Well, let's hope it's tough enough to take it."

"Take what?"

"O.K. may be in for a rough ride. But I guess he's past caring."

The helicopter was hangared in Charlie Site's Silo Number 1. The silo, like its fellows, could be entered from two directions through either the propellant mixing plant or the equipment storehouse. Heaston chose the longer of the two routes. When they reached the storehouse, he motioned Duffy to wait while he scurried down the corkscrew steel staircase which led to the lower tiers of the multi-level cylinder. He reappeared a moment later, panting but triumphant. In his arms was a large olive drab field pack.

"Plastique," he said, giving the explosive its original French pronunciation. "Didn't think Bronko would have enough sense to take it with him." He knelt on the floor to examine the pack's contents. "Yep, still fused and ready. Didn't have to use it on the train because the baggage car wasn't locked, after all. Help me into the straps."

The intercom made them jump. "Get the lead out, Hack," Bronko's voice urged. "We can't wait forever."

"Sounds a mite itchy," Heaston muttered, struggling into the harness. "Take the detonator while I unreel the wire. Fifty feet should be enough." He grasped Duffy's elbow. "You cover me while I plant the plastic—in the Huey if possible, close enough to clip its wings if not. You'll detonate on my signal. When I wave my arm like this, push the plunger. I'll try to be clear by then. Make sense?"

"Not even a little bit. What makes you think they'll let you get close enough to place the bomb?"

"Call it vanity. They're used to taking my commands, no matter what Bronko says. That goes for Bronko, too. If I'm wrong"—he shrugged—"well, be prepared to come up with a better plan."

Duffy held out his hand. "I wish to God I could have known you under different circumstances, Colonel."

Heaston's fingers gripped his tightly. "We're two of a kind, all right." And then he grinned. "Let that be a warning to you, Jake."

Duffy followed him into the short tunnel which led to Silo Number 1, careful to keep the proper distance between them. Ahead in the brilliant rectangle of light was visible the aft two thirds of the waiting helicopter, resembling a painting badly framed. Heaston strode toward it confidently, the detonating wire trailing from the knapsack on his back like the string of a kite. The clatter of the slowly rotating blades blotted out lesser sounds, but Duffy suspected that he was whistling.

Bronko appeared in the tunnel's mouth, peering at the advancing figure. "Hack? Come on—shake a leg!"

"Hack's not coming!" Heaston called back. "Duffy jumped him and they're all dead. I'm going with you."

"Hold it right there, Colonel, or you're dead, too!"

"In a pig's eye!" Heaston scoffed without breaking stride. "I'm not trying to take over command—but you need me and I need you. Quit waving that rifle and let's get out of here."

The bluff succeeded; sergeant faced colonel and the sergeant capitulated. Bronko lowered the carbine slowly. "Okay, hop in. But remember who's running this outfit." Suddenly he took a step backward. He had seen the knapsack with its dangling wire and, seeing, recognized its purpose. "You son of a bitch!" he screamed. Simultaneously, he shot Heaston twice in the chest.

As Heaston fell, Duffy charged, aiming the burp gun. The trigger refused to budge. The mechanism had jammed; with a curse, he strove to clear it. Yet if the burp gun was worthless as a weapon, it was still a shield. The bullet meant for his body struck the gun instead, wrenching it from his grasp. He dived after it. Bronko's second shot passed harmlessly above his head. He rolled over rapidly to evade a third bullet.

It did not come. Bronko, unable to estimate the enemy's strength or capability in the dim light, abandoned his exposed position and vanished from sight. His goal was apparently the auxiliary control panel.

Duffy scrambled forward, intent on reaching the same objective, only to flatten himself again as the men aboard the helicopter filled the tunnel mouth with rifle fire. Pinned down by the barrage, he could merely cower helplessly while the bullets ricocheted from the concrete floor and steel walls. The elevator commenced to rise.

Then, as he lay watching the escape he was powerless to prevent, he saw Anthony Heaston rise also. Despite his wounds, despite the heavy knapsack on his back, Heaston began to crawl, lurching like a mortally injured crab. He clasped the ascending platform with both hands. For an instant he clung to it, all strength drained; then, with a final incredible effort, he pulled his body aboard. His contorted face turned back toward the tunnel, his glazed eyes sought Duffy. As the elevator bore him upward and out of sight, his arm lifted in the signal they had agreed upon.

Duffy's hand closed on the detonator . . . and froze there. I can't, he thought despairingly. At the same instant he heard a voice—his or another's, he could not be sure—say: You must! The wire was already drawing taut. Another second would see it severed. He shut his eyes as if to pray, and pressed down upon the plunger.

The detonation deafened him, the shock wave sent him sprawling. The first explosion was followed immediately by a second, more powerful, which caused the earth itself to quake. The helicopter's fuel tank had ignited. Duffy was showered with burning bits of debris. High above, a writhing fireball, belched from the mouth of the silo as though from a cannon, hung for a moment in the sky like a miniature sun, then died away.

The ponderous elevator, constructed to withstand an even greater blast, was still ascending. Blinded by smoke, Duffy could not find the proper levers on the control board to halt it. He scrambled up the steel ladder, the rungs searing his hands, to join it at the surface.

Devastation awaited him. Of the helicopter, what remained was blackened and twisted wreckage barely recognizable. Of its crew, even less remained and this human wreckage was beyond recognition. Of Anthony Heaston there was no trace whatever. Only the casket of phosphor bronze had survived the twin explosions. Crumpled and dented but still intact, the coffin lay on its side in the shambles, the flag which draped it charred and smoking, like a smoldering log amid the ashes of a gutted campfire.

Duffy stood beside Leslie on the portico of the Orrin Kell Carson Library and watched the sky grow pink with dawn above the Sacramento Mountains. Across the grassy esplanade which was the hub of the Memorial, three black automobiles, one a hearse, waited silently before the pink marble chapel.

The chapel doors swung open. A detachment of soldiers marched out to form an aisle through which a second group descended the steps. The two women and four men—one of whom, oddly enough, carried a camera—entered the first limousine. The honor guard entered the other. Led by the empty hearse, the procession moved slowly down the drive past the Library. Neither mourners nor guards glanced at the two spectators on the portico.

No sooner had the somber caravan departed than a second appeared to take its place. Escorted by more soldiers, two cement trucks pulled up before the chapel, their massive drums rotating. Workmen descended swiftly.

Duffy sighed. "I guess it's all over." Official photographs would prove that the old hero had reached his final resting place. Six feet of concrete would guarantee his slumber there for all time.

"How do you feel, Jake?"

"Okay. Tired, of course."

"No," she insisted. "I mean, how do you *feel?*"

He took a long time to answer. "Older," he said at last. "And maybe wiser. At least, I'd like to think so."

"Is that all? No sense of triumph in having done the impossible?"

He shook his head. "It cost too much. Seven lives—maybe eight, if I count Mindy Queen and I think I can—and for what, actually?"

"You recovered General Carson's body."

"Seven live bodies for one dead one. Was it worth it? I'm not sure O.K. would have thought so. Oh, maybe Bronko and Hack got what was coming to them—but the rest weren't really bad men. They didn't deserve to die. The truth is that I sacrificed them to my ego, simply because I couldn't stand to lose. That's been the story of my life, Leslie. I learned tonight that it isn't enough. There must be a better reason for living. I've got to try to find it."

"Do you think you can? It's not that easy to change."

"The last thing Heaston said to me was that we were two of a kind. He called it a warning. I hope I can heed it—because if I don't I'll wind up the same way he did. I suppose he had a chance to change too, a long time ago, and he muffed it." He regarded her curiously. "Tears?"

"Well, why not? If you're going to act like a real man, let me act like a real woman. And I'll be eternally grateful if you don't make me propose to you!"

Duffy put his arms around her. "Eternal gratitude is too much to expect from a wife. I'll settle for undying affection." After a moment, he mused, "I could probably have my job back if I ask. Upp owes me that much. But I don't think I want it. A lawman has too many opportunities to play God, and I need to break the habit.'

"You have your nerve," Leslie said with mock indignation. "Asking me to marry you when you can't even support a wife."

"Oh, I'll let you support me, at least for a while. Equal rights for women, you know."

"Think you've got it made, don't you? Wouldn't you be surprised if I turned out to be an old-fashioned dependent female, after all?"

"I never make a mistake." He smiled. "Well, almost never."

> The moral's this: Don't you be too proud,
> And don't challenge God (least, not too loud!)
> Or you'll sure wind up like Hub McBain,
> And the iron he called The Gravy Train.
>
> —The Ballad of The Gravy Train